LIFE IN THE WAKE:
FICTION FROM POST-KATRINA NEW ORLEANS

NOLAFUGEES.COM
JOE LONGO, JARRET LOFSTEAD, EDITORS
CHRISTINE P. HORN, ASSOCIATE EDITOR

COVER PHOTO BY ANDY LEVIN
WWW.ANDYLEVIN.COM
BOOK DESIGN AND TYPOGRAPHY BY J. LOFSTEAD

NOLAFUGEES.COM
NEW ORLEANS

OCTOBER 2007

WWW.NOLAFUGEES.COM

LIFE IN THE WAKE:
FICTION FROM POST-KATRINA NEW ORLEANS

NOLAFUGEES.COM

JOE LONGO, JARRET LOFSTEAD, EDITORS

CHRISTINE P. HORN, ASSOCIATE EDITOR

CONTENTS

Foreword

Water. Beginning and end of life in New Orleans. Just as floodwater seeped into places even light could not go, Katrina's aftermath found the weaknesses of any relationship and drove in the wedges. Much as we like to brandish the cliché that the storm brought us together—and it did on many collective levels the world over—it tore us apart on individual levels just as easily. And it is with these conflicts of the heart, within ourselves, our relationships, our communities, our city, that the artist finds fertile ground, not only for relief by fitting the conflict into words, but healing by sharing those words. Maybe, someday after enough of this, we can get on to other business. But for the foreseeable future, Katrina will irrevocably frame all we create.

Within months after the levee failures, a consequence of wetlands erosion, a catastrophe we cannot blame on a foreign enemy, news companies cranked out the first spate of Katrina books, admirable yet rushed picture-filled accounts based on scattered topics and locations. Within a year came the second wave—more informative, researched and searching studies from journalists, historians, and scientists—publications that helped sustain Katrina in the national, and international, consciousness and conscience. The setting was in place.

Then it came time for story. It took almost two years before Katrina's human face emerged in memoir and oral history. And now, with the second anniversary behind us, with this very book, begins the final incarnation, the highest evolution of post-K lit. Fiction.

And through it we find something new in place of all lost. In those first weeks after the levee failures, I stumbled endlessly through shrinking puddles, though ash-gray empty shells of neighborhoods, their only colors the fluorescent spray paint, postmodern skull and cross bones, neighborhoods I never had the chance to know, and ones that I stupidly feared would never again inspire stories, in which only The End cried out to be written.

This new American landscape has not changed much since the levee failures. Place in much of New Orleans has become a shadow of what we once knew. But the writers in this anthology have returned to brave and mine these landscapes, physical and spiritual, and map them for the first time here.

They wallow in the dirty places, those that many people would rather not confront inside themselves, rather not see and choose not to see even as they drive through them, do not look down from the overpass on their way to another island of civilization, do not walk to despite living blocks from them, the ones they think are dangerous despite the fact that they are undergoing natural habitat restoration.

While most people are still reeling, and too many artists don't know where to start because they're just trying to figure out what the hell happened in 2005, these writers are the ones with the elephant-sized balls that charge at our new monsters, however fearfully or fearlessly, crack them in the skull and bare the gray matter for us to see.

NOLAFugees, of course, has long had balls. They were the first to provide a forum for humor after the levee failures. After all, our culture has always put a smile on the face of death. Like those old Mardi Gras masks, we balance the tear in our eye with a smile on our lips.

There's not much humor out there about other disasters. Lampooning the collapse of the twin towers—a precise, single wound inflicted by a precise, single enemy—would be met with righteous protest. By the time we began really understanding what was happening in New York that day, it had already happened. Katrina, however, will be happening for the rest of our lives. We have to joke about it, to make art from it, in order to survive it. Because it's a way of life. Indeed, for many, it is life now.

I met a guy in St. Bernard who, after rescuing over 1500 people from attics and roofs with officials nowhere in site, would fry chicken every evening for them in the local high school cafeteria he had broken into, and entertain everyone with a life-size cutout of Emeríl he found there—"See, here, in this photo, I was asking him if the chicken was cooked yet or if it had enough seasoning on it," he told me outside The Dog House on St. Bernard Highway. "Here he is talking about his seasoning that he had. But I had the Zatarain's right here, you know. I told him, 'I'm using Zatarain's.' Well we sitting there arguing about the seasoning, you know. He wanted to use his. I wanted to use mine. Anyway, after I rescued everybody, I left Emeríl at the high school. He was just too big. Hey, we were happy. We had fun. We made the most of it, you know?"

I think NOLAFugees knows. And they still are making the most of it.

Humor. That quality unique to humans, the ultimate survival mechanism, the key to maintaining sanity in an insane city, the first obstacle against depression, suicide, heart failure. New Orleans is sick. And though we're still crawling along, heart beating strong, the city, with its intermittently vanished neighborhoods, feels to me like an amputee. But at least, with these stories, we can now feel its phantom sensations.

—Joshua Clark

Editors' Note: It is What it Is

In June, 2007, as the first waves of real summer descended on the city, the senior staff of NOLAFugees.com met to discuss our future. As anyone who's ever ground out a summer here will tell you, the verdant months are, to put it nicely, a time of introspection in New Orleans, akin to the deepest Yankee winter. While many have mused on our summer's languid, tropical charm, on the margins of the city, it is traditionally a time of anxiety: murder is high, jobs are short. It is the time that, if you can, you leave; if you can't, you reflect on what you've done wrong, what's prevented you from leaving to finer climes.

A year and a half had passed since our city's undoing and once again we'd entered hurricane season, bringing with us all the excess baggage we'd acquired in the exile of 2005. We'd translated that extra weight into almost two years of writing on NOLAFugees.com, our own chronicle of life in New Orleans, post-Katrina. We'd put the best of the first year into Year Zero and published it. We'd lived in the aftermath of the greatest urban disaster in the history of the world's most powerful nation.

But what were we doing here? In the papers, we'd all read about the host of young, ambitious and generally ennobled individuals who had recently arrived to save New Orleans from itself. From the nation's finer institutions these dedicated, purposeful instruments had come empowered by hope; they saw all the potential of the city's reconstruction. Artists, writers, educators, entrepreneurs: people with vision.

With this, we could not compete. We'd been here too long, had lived too hood-rich, to be so ambitious. Instead, we decided to publish a book composed of short fiction. By word of mouth we solicited manuscripts from New Orleans writers, known and unknown, here and away. Some already had them finished; many said "I don't have a manuscript," and we asked them why they didn't.

We set a deadline, it passed again and again, and these are the stories we have. After two years living in the wake of the hurricane, this great social experiment, with its soft-shoe race politics, its oblique corruption, its half-destroyed landscape and post-diluvian economic stress has produced a single phrase that's on the lips of anyone who's lost a thing to this new life: "it is what it is." It is ching-ming, proper naming, and sums up best the shared experience that came ashore on August 29th, 2005. Every citizen of Orleans Parish, from the lowest in the Nine to the highest in Audubon Place, from Lake Gentilly to the fortress of Algiers, has heard these words passed as they surveyed the new narratives of their lives.

It is what it is, and these stories are what they are, as are their authors. They range wildly; many are grim, some are benign. They are the product of life in the wake of Hurricane Katrina.

Joe Longo, J. Lofstead
Editors, NOLAFugees.com

SHINGLED ISLAND
Joel Farrelly

The rain has stopped and the sun is now beating down unbearable yellow heat. The harsh golden radiance shimmers across the top of the deep stagnant water that laps at the sides of my house, just below the second story roof and I have to turn away as the patchwork of sunrays across the water's opaque brown surface reflects back up into my face.

The rain has stopped, bringing in its wake a sky so clear and vast and blue, it seems almost mocking, and air so thick with humidity it feels like I've been enveloped in a cocoon of hot, wet snakes that are slowly making their way down my throat.

The rain has stopped.

But it's not like that makes things any better.

Here, on the black shingled island of what used to be 6301 Argonne Street, New Orleans, Louisiana, 70124, I'm sitting with my naked legs spread out and baking in the harsh sunlight, a damp T-shirt wrapped around my head, the strap of a black, pump-action shotgun slung over one bare shoulder and I'm staring down at a handful of tiny green pills while I run through the list of reasons why I shouldn't just swallow all of my mother's OxyContin now

Not my mother's, I remind myself.

My dead mother's.

And right there the list gets shorter.

***

Here's me two days ago before the rain, saying "no" when I should have said "yes" to a beautiful girl named Ida on the other end of a phone line, her sweet gentle voice in my ear begging me to leave the city today. Begging me to drive to her father's house in Dallas where I can get a good job and go to school with her. Begging me to say "fuck you" to this entire god-forsaken city.

Here's the sobbing sound she makes when I tell her I can't leave my mother's house and she tries to say something like "please, Milo, don't..." but it all comes out as one combined, wet moan.

Here's a man in a grey suit, standing four inches tall on the television screen in my living room, looking at me through somber eyes as he motions towards the large computer graphic of a multi-colored spiral projected behind him, a vast mess of greens and yellows and reds that keeps swinging across the screen as it leaps from the Gulf of Mexico onto the coast of Louisiana and then over my home which is spelled out in white text as "New Orleans" and then the graphic, which looks more like some child's spin-art catastrophe than a natural disaster, jumps back down to the bottom of the screen and, once again, repeats the process of plowing through everything I know and here's me grabbing the remote from off of the coffee table and aiming it at the whole mess, making it all blink away with a single static hiss as I try desperately not to sound terrified while I tell my girlfriend, whom I haven't seen in three months, who I don't know now that I'll never see again, that I'm sure it's not going to be as bad as people are making it sound and here's her crying louder as I remind her that maybe she shouldn't be so concerned about someone who can't even honestly say he loves her anymore, not after the shit she pulled this summer, and here's the tears finally spilling over and trailing down my face as she says my name like a question and I hang up.

I take one of the OxyContin and swallow it dry as I glance over at the dented plastic Kentwood water jug that sits on the roof next to a half empty box of stale Cap'n Crunch, a dried-out bucket of white paint, the wooden handle of a brush sticking out from its open lid, and an un-zipped backpack containing a folded pair of jeans, two balled-up pairs of socks, a flashlight, spare batteries, a paperback copy of Stephen King's *It*, a butane lighter shaped like a small brass revolver, three packs of Camel lights, a two-carat diamond engagement ring, and about half an ounce of low-grade marijuana. I'm down to about three inches worth of hot chalky-tasting drinking water and the thick wet heat that clings to every inch of me isn't making it any easier not to drink.

Fuck, why didn't I grab more water?

Or at least the rest of the rum?

I drop the remaining pills back into their bottle and snap the childproof lid closed. Then, reaching over, I grab my backpack and put the bottle into the top pocket and then I'm pulling out one of the packs of cigarettes and the butane lighter. My plan is to lie back and smoke a Camel while I wait for the pill to dissolve in my stomach acid and enter my bloodstream but the air is too thick and my throat too dry and when I inhale the cigarette smoke I immediately start coughing. I'm too annoyed to even think of saving the rest of the cigarette and instead angrily flick it past the edge of the roof and I'm expecting to hear the satisfying hiss as the lit Camel lands on the surface of the water but the sound doesn't come.

I tilt my head as I squint down at the blind spot between the roof's gutter and the endless brown water where the cigarette has landed.

Why didn't it hiss?

I pull the damp T-shirt from off of my head and begin to crawl slowly on my hands and knees down the angled slope of the roof, the butt of the shotgun that hangs from my shoulder scraping noisily across the sandpaper-like surface. I reach the end of the roof and grip the edge tightly with both hands as I lean over the metal gutter and look down.

I blink twice and it's still there, floating in the dark water.

Regardless, I blink again.

Just to be sure.

Less than a foot down from my face, my cigarette is burning a dark wound into the fleshy red back of a naked corpse.

The man, from what I can tell, was probably in his mid to late forties and his bloated sun-scorched body that rocks gently against the side of my house shows no signs of decomposition, so I'm thinking he probably hasn't been dead for very long.

I stare down at this stranger's lifeless carcass, one side of its puffy face pressing against the top of what used to be my bedroom window, my cigarette still lit and turning the spot on his back into a small charred crater, and I think about Simon and the night he had asked for something awful.

Here's me, two months ago, sitting at my computer, reading for about the twentieth time an e-mail that Ida had sent, saying how sorry she was, saying she knew how wrong it had been to keep something like that from me, swearing that from now on there would be no secrets between us, telling me that she missed me every second of every day, and reading the words to myself my heart breaks all over again and I know that I can't not forgive her, that I could never stop loving her, and I'm thinking that I should call her, call her right now, this second, and tell her that it's okay, that I'm over the whole thing and it's while I'm holding my cell phone in my hand, starring down at the words "Ida Cell" in my contact list and hesitating as I strain to remember her smiling up at me that first night oh so long ago in some stranger's living room when my bedroom door opens.

Here's Simon, one of my all-time best friends, a pale skinny kid standing in my doorway, looking like an extra in a Weezer video with his shaggy blonde hair, blue hoodie sweatshirt, and black thick-framed glasses. He's leaning against my doorframe, hands in his pockets, saying what's up and asking if I have any of my mom's stuff for sale, meaning OxyContin. And this should seem strange to me because even though I make ends meet middle-manning various narcotics, Simon has never bought anything off of me besides pot. In fact he's probably never in all his years of recreational drug use taken an actual pill before. He was always talking about how pharmaceutical painkillers were the worst kind of drug and how they killed more famous artists than heroin and cocaine combined.

And now here's Simon asking me for OxyContin, the worst of the worst, a synthetic opiate so strong its high rivals smack.

And here's me so caught up in my own little melodramatic microcosm that I don't even ask why he wants them. I don't register the faraway look in his eyes that others would later claim was there all night. I don't say anything and I just sell him the pills, seven of them, 560 milligrams, and then he's moving back through the open

21

door, disappearing into the darkness of the upstairs hallway.

Here's me later that night, moving through a crowd of people I barely recognize, all of them standing around my living room, drinking from bottles of beer and babbling to each other about nothing that could possibly matter when I spot Simon across the room and I can't help but laugh. He is sitting on my sofa, his head tilted back against the wall, looking like he's asleep, but I can't be sure because of the yellow piece of paper that is taped to his forehead, hanging down over his face.

It's why I laugh.

Written on the paper, in black marker, are the words "FUCK THIS."

Here's me, that same night, back in my room, looking down at the girl lying under me on my bed whose name I've already forgotten and she's just soft white skin and round red lips and as I'm fucking her she starts moaning my name and I can feel her spreading wetness dampening the inside of my thighs with each thrust of my pelvis but every time I close my eyes I see Ida's face and I can't come so I eventually stop trying and just roll off of her without a word and wipe my soaked groin on my black bedspread and pass out.

Here's me the next morning or afternoon really, waking up and finding the girl gone and when I eventually go downstairs to smoke a cigarette, I see Simon still asleep on the couch in my now empty living room, "FUCK THIS" still hanging over his face and it makes me smile again as I sit down next to him on the sofa and put on a DVD.

Here's me, later, waking up to film credits rolling slowly across my television screen, realizing that I must have fallen back asleep while watching the movie and the dim, orange light of a sun at dusk shining through the living room's blinds tells me that I've now slept through most of the day and when I turn to look at Simon and I see that he's still asleep I grin and say his name as I try to shake my friend awake and that's when I feel how stiff his arm is through the sleeve of his sweatshirt and then his cold body is falling against me and my smile is fading as I realize that "FUCK THIS" was Simon's own witty attempt at a suicide letter.

He was always so fucking clever when it came to shit like that.

The one good thing about the air being so thick and humid and still is that there's no breeze to prevent me from rolling a joint on the roof of my house. I've turned away from the direction of the dead man's floating remains, not wanting to catch an even accidental glimpse of his bloated scarlet body, and I'm using what little spit I have in my dry mouth to lick the adhesive glue of the rolling paper, quickly sealing the joint closed and placing it between my lips. I light the end and inhale the sweet smoke, holding in my hit, closing my eyes and picturing the capillaries that line the insides of my lungs expanding, being forced to take in the harsh grey cloud I've just sucked down, sending the THC shooting through my bloodstream and enveloping my brain in a thin film of hazy bliss.

I exhale, coughing loudly for several moments and then the coughing becomes a forceful hacking and then I'm spitting out a thick wad of phlegm that lands a few feet away on the hot, shingled surface of the roof. I stare down at the tiny, grey blob for several moments and then I'm bringing the joint back up to my dry lips and taking another drag.

I smoke half the joint before my world dims to the desired level and I put it out, smothering the red cherry between thumb and index finger. My mouth and throat now feel like they're lined with cotton and I can't help but take a small sip from the Kentwood jug. My eyelids lower as I let the warm wetness slide down my dry esophagus and then I'm digging out a handful of Crunch Berries and eating them slowly as I stare up at the vast sky that surrounds me, a sky so wide and so perfectly blue that I'm suddenly filled with the sensation of falling, falling upwards into it and I want to struggle as the azure atmosphere envelopes me, want to tense against it but my limbs feel numb and hollowed out and within moments the sky is swallowing my half-naked sun-burned body whole.

I'm pulled back by the sound of a distant humming.

I know the sound and I should be excited.

It's a helicopter and it's close.

I should be hopping up and down and waving my hands to try and signal for rescue.

I should be laughing and screaming and drinking down the rest of my stale Kentwood water in one satisfying gulp but I don't.

Instead, I remain hunched over, still and silent as I see my mother's eyes slowly closing and the hum of the helicopter fades.

Here's me, maybe yesterday, maybe a lifetime ago, running up carpeted stairs, taking them two at a time as I move quickly towards the second floor of my house and I can still hear the woman's calm, certain voice echoing from downstairs through the speakers of a battery-powered am radio, repeating facts to an empty living room.

The 17th street canal has breached the levee.

The water will be spilling into Lakeview in a matter of moments.

And here's my feet moving me across the upstairs hallway towards my mother's bedroom and here's my hand pressing against the cold metal of a doorknob and here's my wrist twisting as the knob turns and my elbow unbending as the door swings inward and my eyelids blinking in the dim light and my nostrils inhaling swirling dust and the rain outside screaming down as God hurries to reclaim His swamp.

Here's me now standing still in the open doorway as my chest heaves and my eyes scan the white linen landscape of my mother's unmade bed, the comforter and sheets still hanging over one side of the exposed mattress from last week when the EMT had lifted her up and her limp leg had snagged them and now I'm looking away as I move to the night stand and kneel down and I'm about to pull the top drawer out when my cell phone vibrates in my left pocket and I pull it out and read the text message Ida has just sent and it says something about the levees and Lakeview and that she loves me and my cell phone asks if I want to send a reply message and I lie to it and click the END button as my eye catches the image of an eleven year-old boy with shaggy black hair and bright blue eyes, his smile frozen behind thin glass inches from my face and as I blink away a tear and my own distorted image comes into focus, drained and straight-lipped, reflected across the picture's surface, I realize that I am now sitting on the edge of my mother's bed, a hand unconsciously running along the dip in the mattress where she had laid and agonized for months and I grab the framed picture of myself as a young boy from off of the night stand and lay it, face down, in my mother's dent and then I'm standing as I finally pull the drawer open and the round bottle of OxyContin comes rolling into view.

Here's me exiting my mother's bedroom and the blurred series of moments that follow.

Here's the roar of rushing water that envelopes everything.

Here's me grabbing my backpack from my room and stuffing it full of supplies that I had gathered the day before and here's me moving across the hallway to my mother's bedroom where I make sure that her door is securely closed and here's me passing the stairway and glancing down to find that a lake of black water has replaced the first floor of my house and here's me gliding across my room, past my computer and my posters and my bed and my DVDs and the map of the United States that I had made in the fifth grade and here's me sliding, legs first, through an open window and here's me bracing a foot on the window's exterior ledge, warm rain immediately soaking through my clothes as I strain to reach upwards and here's me gripping the rough edge of the roof as I pull myself up and here's me turning to sit on the end of the roof with my legs dangling over the gutter, panting heavily as I stare down at the rapidly rising sea that has replaced the length of Argonne Street.

And here's me watching, the rain beating down on me in sheets, as the water swallows my home.

The helicopter is now directly overhead and so there's no more trying to ignore it. Using a hand to shield my face from the propeller's wind, I look up at the red rescue chopper as it hovers less than twenty feet above me and, spotting the National Guard soldier leaning out from the open side, I force a smile and a quick wave and then immediately wonder why I did so.

I mean, it's not like they don't already obviously see me, so why did I suddenly feel obligated to wave?

Or smile?

I can't possibly believe that these soldiers, finding a half-naked civilian sprawled out on his roof, dehydrated and surrounded by ten feet of cesspool in every direction, would expect some kind of show of appreciation from him.

In fact, I'd bet they're pretty much *expecting* me to be a little pissy.

And, realizing this, my own bitter self-loathing actually begins to lessen.

A voice that might as well be God's booms down from above, "Leave your weapons on the roof! Only take your bag if it ways less than five pounds."

And then the yellow rope ladder is unraveling down at me.

All on their own my hands reach out and grab the ladder and, once again, I'm falling upwards into the blue sky, this time letting it swallow me whole without protest as I glance down at my little shingled island and spot the "FUCK THIS" written across it in white paint and I grin to myself as I think about how much I can't help but agree.

THE LEAST RESISTANCE
Sarah K. Inman

Like water, Chanda followed the path of least resistance. She walked down the back stairwell as she did each morning, and paused by the boarded up window, where most days she would look out at the yard. Sometime during the storm, part of the plywood had blown away from the glass it protected, creating a small enough space for Chanda to peer through. A massive severed oak limb changed the landscape of the backyard. It crushed the garconcier and took down a banana tree. From above, she could see a portion of the oak tree limb had fallen with such force that it had impaled itself on the wrought iron fence. Chanda could tell by looking that a weaker fence would have crumbled beneath the weight of the tree. Oddly enough, an angle existed between the fence and limb, and the rose bushes that lined the gate were spared. While their branches appeared slightly tattered from the wind, their roots held solidly. Spared, too, was the house.

This morning's air was different; it felt cooler than usual, drier, and cleaner, as if the earth breathed a sigh of relief. The storm had knocked out power to the estate, and the generator only provided enough cooling for part of the house, the most important room being where the Old Woman slept. It was only a matter of time, Chanda knew, before one had too much, before one's skin began to wrinkle and curl back into itself. It was only a matter of time before work needed to be done to eliminate the flaws, smooth out the lines. The Old Woman had already had a number of procedures to correct these flaws. In addition to the skin on her face, the Old Woman had work done to her body, which was not functioning well these days. The Old Woman had a disease called diabetes for which she needed daily injections. Chanda understood from the television shows about hospitals that sometimes people who looked like the Old Woman fell asleep and never woke up again. Usually the family members were sad, and sometimes they argued over the estate. Sometimes the husband seemed bereaved, sometimes relieved, and sometimes, as with the Old Woman, there was no man anymore. Chanda knew little of the Old Man, only that he had left the estate before Chanda was born.

The parquet floors echoed with each step Chanda took, and it was dark like when they boarded up the place just a month ago for a storm named Cindy. Chanda recalled the wind that day and the lost power. It was one of the few times she heard the Old Woman telephone Entergy herself to complain about the lack of service. Normally, someone else handled that. The personification of storms befuddled Chanda a little, though she liked what they called this last one, Katrina, since she once had a dog by the same name. Katrina, the deceased yellow lab, lay buried in the backyard beneath the surviving rose bushes.

When Chanda reached the ground floor, she walked outside into the sunshine. Except for the generator's hum, the air was strangely silent. On mornings when the weather was nice, she liked to sit on the tree swing and pump herself back and forth until breakfast, but today the swing lay beneath the fallen oak limb. Chanda crouched down on all fours and tugged at the wooden swing. Though not a large woman, Chanda's arms and core were made strong through yoga. Walking and swimming kept her lower body fit. Chanda exhaled forcefully as she yanked the swing from beneath the tree, scraping her arm along a branch and landing in the mud on her sit bones. Tied to the branch, the swing would go no further. Still, Chanda gave it a quick tug. Truffle, the estate's long-haired black cat, followed Chanda through the sun porch to the kitchen, where she went to retrieve a knife.

Inside, the nurse's aid sat at the counter punching numbers into her cell phone.

"Chanda, baby," LaKesha spoke. "What happened to you? And where you going with that knife?"

"My swing is stuck." The cat rubbed against her legs and trotted to its food dish.

"No swinging today, baby. You be careful with that, and come straight back inside, you heard? I got something important to tell you."

Knife in hand, Chanda approached the fallen branch. The ground around her feet was soggy from the rain. More mud collected on her feet and ankles. The leaves of the camellia bushes along the side of the house had been flipped inside out by the wind, their lighter undersides now exposed, and the flowers themselves were blown away, all except for one small tough bud that was spared. It was strange what plants survived the wind and which ones did not. The magnolia's trunk had snapped in half, but the oleander bushes remained.

Chanda breathed in the damp scent of the river and the fragrant gardenia, another survivor; the leaves scattered about the yard with everything else. Natural gas and the smell of something burning reached her senses too.

In the distance a dog barked, but no human sound came her way, no traffic, no voices. Then, from above, there came the whir of a helicopter. The buzz increased as it moved closer and flew low to the ground as if it wanted to land on the house. For a while, Chanda stood with her eyes to the sky, watching the mechanical bird fly, rattling the tops of trees as it followed its course. Once again, Chanda moved through the obstacle course of fallen branches toward her swing, occasionally being scratched. Using the knife, she severed the swing's ropes, and pulled it from beneath the branch. The swing's lines were limp and still wet from the rain. Chanda wrapped the ropes around the flat wooden seat and brought her favorite toy inside.

"Chanda, baby," LaKesha spoke as Chanda approached. "I made us some eggs. We still got gas, you know."

"Thank you so much, Miss Kesha," Chanda answered as she took a seat at the breakfast nook. "May I have some orange juice, please?"

"Chanda, baby," LaKesha said softly. "You know the Old Woman ain't been feeling too good for a while now."

"Mmm, umm," Chanda nodded.

"And you know that everybody's day must come? That the Lord calls on us all. Someday he'll call on me and someday he'll call on you."

"Yes, I know."

"Today or last night, the Lord called on the Old Woman, and now we pray she's resting with Jesus."

"She's resting with Jesus," Chanda repeated. She stood up, opened the refrigerator, which failed to light up usual, and pulled out a carton of orange juice. Chanda recalled that LaKesha was a home care provider, not a maid, and she'd been told more than once to get her own cold drinks.

"I've been trying to call on someone to come and get the body, but it's no getting through. The lines are down, and my cell ain't working. Do you know where your old lady's phone is at? We need to call someone to get her body. Do you understand?"

"Yes ma'am," Chanda answered. She understood that people carried phones with them nowadays. Back when she was small, people made phone calls from home or from the street corner, but today people talked on the phone while in their cars, on sidewalks, and in stores. Chanda even recalled a woman who talked on the phone while in a restaurant's toilet stall. Chanda pointed to the bright yellow phone that matched the kitchen décor and was bolted to the room's wall.

"You poor thing," LaKesha began. "The lines been down since we lost power. No dial tone, baby." She picked up the receiver and held it out for Chanda, who stared back at the appliance. "No dial tone," LaKesha repeated.

"Phone's out," Chanda said.

"Who's gonna look after you?" LaKesha asked. "Look at that; you got mud all over your feet."

Chanda looked at her dirty feet and ankles. The mud felt cool but itchy.

"I suppose the mess don't matter now," LaKesha said.

When Chanda finished her breakfast, she followed Miss Kesha upstairs to the Old Woman's bedroom, which felt cooler than the rest of the house. The closed blinds cast an orange glow to the place. Chanda stepped to the bed. Beneath the canopy lay the Old Woman, tucked into her sheets as if she were merely asleep on her back, except her eyes were wide open. They stared up at the ceiling, two blue orbs surrounded by freshly tucked skin.

"I tried to shut her eyes, but they won't stay closed," LaKesha said.

The Old Woman's legs, thin as the bedposts, shaped the blanket that covered her. Her wrinkled hands rested at her sides. In comparison, LaKesha was much larger and darker than the Old Woman. Where the Old Woman's legs matched the bedposts in size, LaKesha's skin matched the wood in color. Though closer in complexion to the Old Woman, Chanda wasn't very pale. A day in the sun turned her skin brown, not pink.

"She looks so peaceful," Chanda said, remembering that this is what people on television often said of the dead.

"No, she don't," LaKesha blurted. "I got to get them eyes shut, and look at her mouth. That won't close neither." LaKesha was right. On television and in the movies when they showed the dead, they sometimes did have open mouths and eyes, but sometimes they didn't. LaKesha stood over the Old Woman and tried pressing the lady's lids down once more, but the Old Woman's eyes, blue like the wading pool, empty like the sky, remained opened. Then LaKesha gently pushed on the Old Woman's jaw, but it too would not stay fully shut. "I give up, girl. You want to show me where her cell phone is at?"

Ever since the baby came, Chanda was allowed in the Old Woman's room more often than before. She led LaKesha to the Old Woman's desk where a cellular phone lay. LaKesha picked up the phone while Chanda wandered back downstairs to try the large television, which still didn't work. Instead, she looked through a magazine about home decorating.

34

***

Without the hum of the central air, Chanda could hear LaKesha from downstairs. She fussed at someone on the phone in a way Chanda could barely understand.

"I got to find my people," LaKesha cried. She ran down the stairs. "I gotta go, baby."

"All right, now," Chanda said, echoing the sentiments of what she heard people say when they calmed one another.

"For real," LaKesha answered. "I ain't playin'. The levees broke, girl. We got to get out of this city. Put some shoes on, and let's go."

"Where?" Sometimes Chanda went to the market with Tammy, the housekeeper, but she never went anywhere with LaKesha.

"Get your things, girl. The levees broke and we in trouble."

In the car, LaKesha asked, "You ain't packed nothing?"

Chanda held the swing in her lap and touched the medal of the Virgin Mary at her neck. "This is all I'll ever need. This and faith," Chanda repeated what the nuns at Ursuline had once told her. Though she never understood what it meant, it seemed like the right answer.

"Yeah, you right. I brought us some water and took some canned goods from the pantry. The rest is in God's hands now."

Chanda hardly recognized St. Charles Avenue with the fallen tree branches, downed power lines, and homes with boarded windows. At other times in her life, she had ventured out after storms to see the green leaves of oak trees littering the streets, scattered to and fro, not unlike the messy beauty of the English gardens she recalled from magazines the Old Woman kept around the house.

Behind the gate of a home larger than the one Chanda spent her life in, she saw a man standing with a big gun across his chest. He positioned himself the way men at the boarders of dangerous places stood with their weapons.

In earlier years when the Old Woman was well, she and Chanda sometimes went to Audubon Park together or shopping on Magazine Street, but Chanda could not recall the streets looking this empty. They weren't even this barren on Ash Wednesday. LaKesha turned off St. Charles Avenue, and the pair headed into a neighborhood unfamiliar to Chanda. The houses got smaller and closer to the street, which was filled with holes that made the car bounce. Each time it rumbled over a hole in the road, the car made an obscene noise. Chanda could feel the vehicle shake, making it seem as if it would simply fall apart.

LaKesha swerved to avoid something and then drove on the wrong side of the road around a fallen traffic light. It lay in the middle of the street, void of power. Every now and then LaKesha would stop the car, get out, and call on Chanda to help her move debris from the road. Still, they saw no people except for the armed guard.

"Don't worry, baby. We going by my sister's place, gonna check on them."

Several more times they had to get out of the car and move debris from their path. Chanda saw houses where weeds had engulfed rooftops, and she wondered about this since she couldn't recall one photo from *House & Garden* looking anything like these places. It took time for things to grow, Chanda knew. In no way was the rooftop vegetation related to the storm. Rusty cars lined the roads. Chanda couldn't recall being in this neighborhood before.

"I ain't never seen this so deserted. Girl, make sure your door is locked," LaKesha said.

Just then a person appeared in the middle of the street. She was darker than LaKesha and her head was wrapped with a red cloth, the same kind of wrap LaKesha wore sometimes when she came to care for the Old Woman.

"Is that your sister?" Chanda asked.

When the woman turned, Chanda saw the child, a toddler, pressed to the woman's hip.

"No, that ain't my sister."

The woman waved one arm and held the child with the other. She hopped up and down, commanding attention. "Please stop. Stop."

Instead, LaKesha accelerated past the woman, and soon there were more people, dark people, like LaKesha. At the sight of the car, they waved; some ran towards it. There were others, too, clusters of dark skinned folks walking with shopping carts. In one cart, Chanda saw two children. Another was piled high with bottles of water and soda. The person pushing it yelled in a language Chanda had heard LaKesha speak. It sounded like when she talked on the phone with her family. They all moved in the same direction, a sea of brown faces.

LaKesha maneuvered the car past buildings hidden beneath the swaying oaks, brick buildings with small windows, a giant layered house of sorts. It was dark and mysterious without the tall windows of the homes in Chanda's neighborhood. Chanda had never seen anything like it in the magazines they kept around the

Old Woman's house, but she knew from watching the news and movies that such places existed. Black people lived in places like these. Some of these people had guns, and many of them smoked from a glass pipe instead of a cigarette. (Ever since the Old Woman had quit smoking, she didn't allow it in the house, and certainly no one in the house ever tried to smoke from a glass pipe.) Chanda knew that the people who lived here used tickets and not dollar bills or credit cards to buy groceries. LaKesha and Chanda passed a fenced-in field, a basketball court where the rims were without nets, and another cluster of concrete buildings. These sat low to the ground. Bars covered the doors and small windows. A group of people gathered around a building with pictures of food painted on its side, a mural-sized muffuletta, a drumstick, a crab and a crawfish. Some restaurants, Chanda knew, put pictures of food on the menus, and she liked this. Otherwise, the Old Woman would order for her. Apparently the building with the pictures of food was locked and no one had a key. Glass littered the ground near the one window and door, as the crowd struggled with the bars. Then a man with a crowbar in his hand came along and pried open the gate to the store. He pushed his way inside ahead of the crowd who followed him.

"They all coming this way," LaKesha noted. "It's a bad sign." She punched numbers into the Old Woman's cellular phone. "The lines is all tied up. I should have told her to head our way instead. It was a miracle I got through in the first place."

Sensing concern in LaKesha's voice, Chanda offered advice she heard in yoga class: "Focus on your breath." Twice a week Chanda dressed in loose clothing and went to a place where she and a group of people did the same physical movements for about an hour and a half. They called it yoga, and though it sometimes pushed her physical limits, she didn't find the experience unpleasant. Whenever one of the participants became concerned or overworked, worried in a way Chanda sensed LaKesha was worried, the instructor reminded the students of their breath.

Despite Chanda's soothing words, LaKesha panicked. "Oh, look out, there's water here." They drove into the shallow waters of an urban lake. Chanda had visited homes on the North shore built around Lake Pontchartrain, but she'd never seen this: homes and businesses on top of water. "Oh, no, we ain't got much further to go, so hold on baby. I got to get my sister."

Chanda couldn't understand what troubled LaKesha so much, even as she realized the threat of rising water, of how it wasn't supposed to be here, in the streets. Chanda remembered the May Flood, the spring before the baby was put in her. She was younger then, when the rain didn't stop and the streets filled with water. She recalled times when she and the Old Woman had been caught out in street floods, but this was different somehow. First, it usually rained, a torrential downpour the newscasters called it, and normally, the sun didn't come out like it did now. Sunshine generally coincided with the water going down, not rising.

"Where's the water coming from?" Chanda asked.

"I don't know, baby. The Lake. The River. Who knows? I got word the levees broke is all. We might be okay by your house, but I have to get my sister. I can't get her on the phone. The lines is tied up."

When the water reached the car's doors, LaKesha lost control of the automobile, and it began to drift despite her efforts at steering. "Baby, we got to get out of this thing," she said. "You know how to swim?"

As a child, Chanda was placed in a pool with other kids her own age and taught to swim. Later in life, when she and the Old Woman would visit the spa at the Ritz for massages, Chanda took advantage of the pool as well as the hot tub and steam room.

Chanda watched as the sun shined and the water rose. The curve of the land, its depletion was now evident. She looked at the Crescent City, and despite its geography, Chanda knew it wasn't usual to have water pouring in while the sun shined. It reminded Chanda of a scene in a movie about the end of the world. To escape the rising tide, some people climbed fences or hopped onto front porches. Others sought refuge on the tops of parked cars, waiting for the surge to subside. Chanda watched people wade through the water, all heading towards her and LaKesha. People swam in their direction, and from a distance they appeared as a group of ducks migrating together, or a fleet of boats, tiny vessels bound for the same destination.

Chanda opened the door as the water seeped through the floor of the car and rushed in around her feet. She stepped onto the flooded street; the water reached her knees. Something live brushed against her leg. Chanda looked down at the shrimp that floated with the incoming tide.

"This way, baby," LaKesha commanded. Chanda grabbed her hand and together they waded across the deluge, walking several blocks through water that varied in depth from knee deep to waist deep. They saw a man playing a guitar on his porch, a woman drinking a beer. A boat captained by a person who carried a pistol in his hand floated past the pair. On a second story balcony, Chanda noticed a family. Five small children danced at the sight of the boat, cried out for help while the mother held an infant in her arms.

To reach LaKesha's sister's house, the pair climbed a set of submerged front steps. Water covered the front porch, and the door was open. LaKesha pushed aside the floating plastic furniture, an end table and a couple of chairs, before entering the house.

"Come on, baby," she said as she led Chanda through the small home. The water reached Chanda's hips and she moved carefully, unable to see where her next step would take her. A funny smell pervaded the living space, a mix of natural gas and chemicals. It smelled a little like after the cleaning woman left the house, but not clean and much stronger. It made Chanda's head ache.

"In the back, baby, the back of the house," LaKesha commanded. It was dark inside since the houses on the street were built so close together, and what little windows they had were barred and covered with curtains. Some of the kitchen cabinets had popped open, and Chanda watched as the water, propelled by LaKesha's wake, lapped up the clutter from the kitchen table, a couple of bowls, silverware, and plastic cups. A child's toy brushed against Chanda's hip.

In the living room the television, sofa and chairs sat half submerged like a cluster of islands. Chanda bumped her knee on something as she waded through the living space.

"Careful, girl," LaKesha offered. Then in a louder voice, she cried out, "We coming. It's me, baby, and we coming."

Despite the darkness, Chanda had little difficulty following LaKesha because the rooms lined up one after another. Only the bathroom didn't follow the row. Instead, it was an offshoot of the hallway. Chanda peered inside and watched as the toilet seat flopped in waves created by their movement. A small animal—a rat perhaps—scurried up the wall and sought refuge on the shower's spigot. Finally, they reached the last room of the house, a bedroom where a cluster of people gathered on a soggy mattress; a young man at the front clutched a gun in his hands.

"It's okay, baby," LaKesha spoke. Though she couldn't determine the exact number of people on the bed, Chanda knew they wouldn't all fit in LaKesha's car, and besides the car had most likely succumbed to the waters by now. The youngest of the bunch, a toddler, cried.

"Who this?" a heavy-set woman demanded. She appeared to have a large one hundred dollar bill pinned to her head, but upon closer inspection, Chanda could tell what wrapped around her skull was not money but a representation of it, a headband in the likeness of currency.

"You know the lady I work for?" LaKesha asked. "Well, she dead, and this the other one who live in the house."

"Oh, no. Things is bad Uptown?" the woman with the money head wrap asked.

"Ain't no water on St. Charles," LaKesha offered. "At least not yet. Soon as I saw the people coming at us and then the water, I been trying to call you, tell you to come our way, but ain't no use. The lines is down."

Staring at Chanda for a moment, the woman with the money wrap said, "You look like that lady on TV."

"What lady?" LaKesha asked.

"You know, that one on the news."

"Yes, indeed," LaKesha said, and that was the last of the conversation Chanda understood fully. LaKesha and her sister spoke quickly in a language that sounded foreign. At the big woman's command, the group on the bed began to exit the house through the back door. The young man with the gun stood up, tucked the weapon into his waistband, and moved in the water by the door; he unhinged a two by four that blocked the door and with some effort, opened it. One by one, he lifted the small children and carried them outside.

LaKesha looked at Chanda and said, "We going back to your place, but we have to walk through this. You heard? The car's out."

Chanda followed the older children out the back door. The young man found couch cushions for the smaller children to float on. The older and taller kids pushed the younger ones through the deep water, which was slick with oil in places. Chanda's head pounded from the fumes, and it occurred to her that today, unlike all other days, she hadn't showered yet. Before setting off into the waters around LaKesha's sister's house, Chanda looked at her reflection in the window and noticed her hair had begun to curl, a natural reaction to the humidity.

"I have this," Chanda pointed to the swing clutched under her arm.

"Go on, now," the young man signaled for one of the smaller children to grab Chanda's swing.

The water wasn't cold by any means, but after a while of walking through it, Chanda began to shiver. As she made her way out of the shadows, she welcomed the warmth of the sunshine.

"I'm tired," the boy next to her said. The water reached his chest. He passed the child who floated on a couch cushion to Chanda. Behind her, she dragged a child on her swing. "Carry me," the walking boy added and then climbed Chanda's back despite his mother's cries of "Get down from there. Walk on your own two feet." The human weight on her shoulders was a mild discomfort, one Chanda simply tolerated. The Old Woman kept Epsom salts and other remedies for sore muscles in the bathrooms back home. Chanda watched as a dog swam past them, his head and neck above water.

The woman with the money on her head, the one LaKesha had introduced as her sister, cried out something unintelligible.

Chanda recalled a phrase her yoga instructor often used when the class assumed a difficult posture and complained about it. "Learn to let go," Chanda said as she moved through Central City's murky waters.

BOURBON STREET
Bill Loehfelm

I parked in the middle of Seventh Street, hitting the hazard flashers before I climbed out of the car. I stretched, trying to work the kinks of a nine-hour drive from Atlanta out of my back. When my spine stopped popping and cracking I realized the muted clicking of the flashers was the only sound on my street. I felt like a fool for turning them on. There was nobody here. Not the casual 'nobody,' like in the middle of a New Orleans summer when the tourists and the college kids disappear and my neighborhood reverts back to the locals, who all exert about as much energy that time of year as a lizard on a rock. There was not another person from Magazine to Prytania and beyond on either side. It didn't matter if I parked in the middle of the street. Didn't matter if I locked the car, or even took the keys out of the ignition. I opened the car door and turned off the hazards.

On a mid-week, late September afternoon, I stood on a city street enveloped in silence. It scared the heart out of me, and I couldn't get my mind around it. This wasn't my first experience with profound silence, and in the past it had comforted me. I often took solace in the fact that such a thing remained possible; I even knew where it happened. Ten years before the summer of Katrina, the winter before I'd moved to New Orleans, I had camped for the night on a rocky outcropping overlooking a moonlit ghost town in Death Valley, California. That night I learned the difference between simple quiet and utter silence.

But the desert was supposed to be silent, the emptiness, the stillness; they were part of the package, part of the definition. City streets were not supposed to be silent. But I couldn't even say my street reminded me of that ghost town. There was the same lack of people, the same abundance of boarded-up windows and punched-out rooftops. The same debris covered streets. But deserts and ghost towns weren't green like my street. Left alone, the elaborate gardens of my neighbors had grown wild and vibrant, each a miniature Eden straining at the gates. The live oaks lining my street were beat to hell but alive. Some still clung to many of their leaves and wore the emerald green of their resurrection ferns like bandages. Maybe that was what unnerved me so. My street felt dead and still, but as I took a deep breath of the hot, pungent New Orleans air, I smelled life everywhere around me.

I made my way to the wrought-iron fence of my landlords' property, stepping carefully the stray roofing tacks the TV had warned me about before leaving Atlanta. Shingles of torn tarpaper and busted slate littered the sidewalk and street all around me, scattered like a deck of cards tossed from a car window. From the fence, though, my landlords' house looked okay. The windows were boarded exactly as I had left them. A columned and galleried Greek-Revival mansion, the house approached the sidewalk in front but had a large yard in back. I lived in a converted pool house in the back, a one-bedroom, four-room cottage that always smelled like burnt coffee and old chlorine. So the Arcenaux house, which had been in the family since that first generation made its fortune through the trade of cotton and the labor of Africans, still stood. The front yard, however, was a different story.

The crepe myrtle that had shaded the porch had snapped in half and toppled over, smashing a few feet of fence on impact. Its smooth, dead branches blocked the driveway. The tree's bright pink flowers and small green leaves pooled half-rotted in puddles of rainwater on the concrete. During the month I'd been away, I hadn't though much about the crepe myrtle; it was the towering palm in the front corner of the yard that had really worried me. If that had gone down it could've taken half the house with it. But the palm wasn't even leaning. Half the fronds were gone, and the remaining half were yellowing and shredded, but the trunk looked as sturdy as ever. It seemed the Arcenauxs had been spared.

I shoved the front gate open far enough to squeeze into the yard. I managed to climb through the crepe myrtle branches onto the pathway to the backyard. As I opened the padlock to the back gate, I felt optimistic about my own fortunes.

From what I had seen, we had gotten off easy. Cleaning up the yard would be a bitch, but what did it matter if that dead tree was left to lie where it fell? There was no saving it. The mailman didn't need to get through; there wasn't one. The neighbors wouldn't complain; there weren't any. When they got back, and who knew when that would be, if they returned at all, they'd have enough problems of their own. Fuck that tree, I thought. And then I turned the corner around the back of the house and into the yard. No, I thought. Fuck me.

The neighbor's giant magnolia had fallen and cut my cottage in half. The trunk lay against the ground, with either side of the smashed building leaning against it. It was a total loss; I could tell just by looking at it. Buried somewhere in the rubble, pulverized by the tree, baked in the sun, and drenched in Katrina's and Rita's rain, was what little I had of my new novel.

Of course, I had a back-up copy of my work on a disk. But I'd left the disk on my desk in the living room, which was also where I'd left my laptop when I packed my overnight bag for a three-day stay in Atlanta. Before I left it never occurred to me that my entire cottage, never mind anything in it, would be reduced to shrapnel while I was away. A lot of people, including all of my neighbors, had thought just like me when evacuating.

I tried to use that thought to forgive myself, but I couldn't. It burned me up inside, thinking about how easily I could've grabbed that disk or even the computer on my way out the door. What fucking purpose had buying a laptop served if I left it behind when I ran for my life? A month ago, though, evacuating hadn't been fleeing for survival. It had been a minor inconvenience. I knew I hadn't been alone in thinking that way. Still, a voice hissed in my head, a *real* writer would never have left his work behind.

The hundred pages I'd written in the three years since grad school hadn't seemed like much. A hundred pages that still needed tons of work in addition to the two hundred or so needed to finish the story. I remembered how embarrassed I was when a friend of mine from the M.F.A. program landed a modest deal for his first novel, telling him a hundred pages was all I had. We'd both had about fifty on graduation day. One hundred pages had seemed barely a toe in the water when I was forced to talk about it. Now, staring at the rubble of not just my writing life but my whole life, those pages seemed liked an unmined vein of gold. It seemed like a world more than what I had now, which was nothing. I knew that my friend hadn't left his work behind.

Light-headed from shock and heat, I wiped the sweat from my face with my shirttails and sat down in the grass. It was already budding and over grown. Looking around at the buzz-cut treetops and torn-up houses around me, I saw no signs of life. No birds, no bugs, no squirrels. I waited and strained to see, or hear, another living animal. Nothing appeared to me. Beads of sweat trickled down my back. I could hear them. I began to fear the sky would show me only ravens and crows, or worse, vultures. I closed my eyes.

I took the press pass from around my neck and tossed it away, wondering if everyone and everything else that had lived in New Orleans, harbingers of doom included, had already come back, packed up and gotten the hell out. I imagined clearly a family of squirrels packing bags into one of those little cars they drive on TV and, sad-faced but resolute, lighting out for a living city. Apparently, I was the only one who hadn't gotten the memo.

At some point, I needed to call the landlords and give them the low down, let them know their life was left standing and mine wasn't. Let them know the huge magnolia tree next door had, against all odds, missed the big house but smashed the little one to bits. That stroke of luck would be a great relief to them. I remembered that back in July they'd raised my rent. I didn't make the call, but I kept thinking about it. I wanted someone, anyone, to explain to me what had happened here. To tell me what to do. Being multi-generational natives, I thought maybe the Arcenauxs would have answers for me.

Because, now that I was sitting in the middle of it, the reality rendered irrelevant the gazillion hours of CNN I had watched over the preceding weeks. Some part of my brain, the modern

American part even New Orleans had yet to undo, must have registered those repeating images of apocalypse as beaming in from Ghana, or Honduras, or Indonesia, or some imaginary conflation of impoverished Third World countries – places where things like killer hurricanes always happened, where they were, a lifetime of TV had taught me, supposed to happen. Places where I was used to seeing, from the safety of a couch, black and brown people filthy and starving in the streets.

During the first days of the flood, watching the Superdome (where I had season tickets), and Canal Street (where I always got caught in traffic), and the Circle Grocery (which I'd always been afraid to go into), and the Rite-Aid on the corner of Napoleon and Claiborne (where I stocked up on Ben & Jerry's) all drown, every single one of them along with hundreds of other places and people, had driven the tragedy home. It had certainly felt that way. Now, sitting there in scratchy weeds and grass, seeing it small scale and up-close, not having seen most or the worst of it, I realized I didn't know a fucking thing about what had happened to New Orleans.

I don't know how long I sat there, but my thoughts had shifted to breaking into the neighbors' houses and stealing all their bourbon when I heard the back gate squeak open. I turned to see two National Guard soldiers in full battle gear, automatic rifles cradled in their arms, approaching me across the yard. They couldn't have known what I was plotting, yet I felt the shame of being caught red-handed.

"Is this your home, sir?" one of them asked. He slung his rifle over his shoulder. He looked about fourteen. "Can I see some ID?"

I nodded and stood, reaching slowly into my pocket for my wallet. I walked over to him and handed over my driver's license. I thought of another wrecked, wasted city: Baghdad.

The soldier looked at my license for a long time and then handed it back to me. "You realize this is still a restricted area?"

"I do," I said. "I'm here on a story assignment. I'm a writer." I looked around in the grass. "I have my press credentials around here somewhere." I hunched over and continued looking, unable to find them. I couldn't have thrown them that far. "I'm here for the *New York Times*."

It was a big, fat lie, and a dumb one. I didn't know why I'd told it. A close read of those credentials would have given me away. My parents back in Jersey talked their neighbor, a features editor for the *Bergen County Record*, into Fed-Exing me a press pass so I could get into the city. He'd probably made it on his computer in five minutes. The headshot was my high school yearbook photo. The guardsman at the city limits had cocked a skeptical eyebrow at my bad tuxedo. At least I hadn't told him I was from *The Times*.

I'd lied to my folks too, telling them I only wanted back in so I could get my stuff and get right back out. Why in God's name had I expended so much energy trying to get back here? I'd had air-conditioning, free booze, and ESPN in Atlanta. I'd had a big room at my brother's house. A bed. A roof. Here, I had the sweats, a backache, and a pile of rubble. My presence in my own yard was under question by boys with guns. I turned to the soldier. If he bought the lie, he wasn't impressed, but he didn't ask for the pass.

"Is that your vehicle out front?" he asked.

"It is."

"We'll need you to move it out of the roadway. In case of fire or a law enforcement action."

I scratched at my chin. "I'm not sure where to put it."

Expressionless, the soldier turned and walked back out front, followed by his partner. They locked their guns in the truck and started clearing the limbs and branches from in front of the house, tossing them into the front yard. I watched for a while then wised up and ran over to help.

When we were done, I pulled the car to the curb, running over several roofing tacks, and locking all the doors before I got out. I thanked the soldiers for their help as they climbed back into their Humvee. They didn't seem to hear the air hissing from one or more of my tires. I did. It sounded really loud. Was there anywhere within fifty miles to get new tires? Even if there was a place, how would I get there? I kicked my left rear wheel. Fuck it, I had no use for goddamn tires, anyway. I'd have run out of gas before I got three blocks away. Bourbon, on the other hand, I had a use for. Would these guys understand if I requested their help in getting some?

Before I could ask, from the passenger side of the Humvee, one of the soldiers handed me a six-pack of canned water and a box of MRE's.

"Heating instructions are on the individual packets," he said. He smiled. "Sorry, no gumbo for you just yet." He seemed to really believe we were only days away from gumbo availability, though served fresh or in a combat zone meal packet I wasn't sure.

"We'll be patrolling the neighborhood, frequently," the other one said.

He'd meant the remark to be reassuring but it felt like a threat. I didn't know why. I had come home to my house in my

54

neighborhood. I lived here. Unless these two, I realized, decided I didn't and revoked my permission to be here. Could they really do that? If I could be told I didn't live here, where did I live? I was terrified that if they told me I didn't live here, they'd be right. What did I have to offer as an argument? The shattered remains of my rental cottage? There was no one around to testify I'd ever lived here at all. From what I could see, no one lived in New Orleans anymore.

I watched the soldiers suspiciously as one unlocked the guns and the other stared blankly ahead from the driver's seat. Where did these guys live? What was home to them? They seemed to think the mansion was mine. That told me they sure as hell weren't from around here. They didn't know anything about this place, other than it was "a restricted area" and that anyone without a uniform and a gun needed a good, hard look.

I wondered if they even knew where they got their shoes at. I had a feeling they didn't. But I did. I'd picked that talent up my first night in the Quarter. For the bargain price of ten bucks a gap-toothed, street corner hustler learned me that where I got my shoes at was Bourbon Street, New Orleans, Louisiana. It was money well spent. That exchange taught me more about New Orleans than anything has since.

The soldiers started their truck. "If you need anything," the passenger said, "flag us down. Just don't approach the vehicle too quickly."

I assured them I wouldn't. I held up my cell-phone. "You guys answer 911?"

"There is no 911," he said.

"And if that's a cell-phone with a 504 area code," said the driver, "it won't work anyway." He nodded at the landlords' house. "Try your landline inside. Every now and then, one turns up that works. You might luck out."

"Thanks," I said. "How long will y'all be around?"

"Quite a while," they said in unison.

"At least till they send us back to Iraq," one said. "Where we're needed." They laughed.

I wondered if anyone in Baghdad, American or Iraqi, knew where they got their shoes at.

The driver looked at me. "There is a dusk-to-dawn curfew in effect. We advise you to stay inside after dark and to not make a lot of noise."

At first, I thought they were referring to my imaginary bourbon thievery. The serious looks on both their faces told me otherwise. But the idea continued gathering steam in my brain. I knew enough about my neighbors to know there was a lot of bourbon to be had, curfew be damned.

"There are bad people still about," one of them said. "People who are trying to take advantage of the difficult security situation here."

I agreed to follow their instructions.

"Is there anything else we can do for you, sir?"

"Where you got your shoes at?" I asked.

They both stared at me for a long time, confused. "Military issue," the one on the passenger side finally said, extending his leg.

"That's exactly the answer I expected," I said to him, nodding my head. It felt comforting to finally get something right. I clutched tighter at my canned water and combat food. Bourbon for all my horses, I shouted in my head.

"Be careful, sir," the soldier replied, slamming the Humvee into gear. "Welcome home."

Thinking Outside of the Box
Ken Foster

Nico says we need to get our numbers up or the whole program's shutting down. That means going back into construction or recovery, or, even worse, going home. Nico's from up north too, so she knows what we're all thinking. We don't want to go back yet, not while it is still cold. Nico's got her palm pilot out. She's making calculations.

"If you can't bring in four a day," she says, "we can't afford you."

Stevie and I look at each other, trying really hard not to register anything. Four is a lot. Especially with all the pit bulls around.

I met Stevie at Johnny White's Sports Bar my first night in town. It was the only place open. That's what the TV said. So there we were in there drinking, wondering where all the locals were. Everyone seemed to be from out of town. Everyone had managed to get in somehow, to get work, to fix things up, even though it wasn't our town.

"Where is everyone?" one of us asked and the waitress gave the same look we'd been getting. That's how you know they lived here before the storm. When they look at you like there's only one reason you'd be here now and they don't like it.

Stevie had had a little too much to drink already, so he started giving her a hard time. "What's wrong with everyone? I gave up my job to come down here and help out. I said goodbye to my friends."

The waitress looked skeptical. "You're down here volunteering?" she asked.

"Yes I am," Stevie said. "Animal rescue." And we got a free round.

Of course, Stevie actually had come down for paid work. But later that night he told me that he figured it out pretty quickly that even though you could make a ton of money clearing debris and then selling off the salvageable stuff, the volunteer stuff paid better in the end. If you were working, people knew you could afford to pay for everything, and with rents being what they were, and most of the buildings still uninhabitable, it was like you were doing all that heavy labor for nothing. But if you volunteered, people gave stuff. More than you could ever need. People sent stuff in from out of town. All you needed to do was show up for your assignment in the morning, come back later and say you tried real hard. They'd hand out food and water and at night they had bunks to sleep in, if you didn't find someone with an empty house you could crash in.

"They took this church," he said. "They converted the pews. It's badass. When we're done with all this, I'm gonna take one of those babies home.

"And the food! You should see those FEMA sandwiches. You can gnaw on one of those for days."

He was right about the food. They were fat with pastrami and cheese, and then they'd toss in a chef's salad too. Meat salad, we called it. Even if we weren't at the base of operations when the FEMA food arrived, there was always the Red Cross to hit, too. The problem was we were supposed to be looking for animals out in the disaster zone, and they weren't coming out there with any food. So we stuck close in until lunchtime.

Once, I wondered aloud if it was strange that they'd been giving us all their food. Stevie scrunched up his face. "It's hard out there," he said. He meant the parts of the city where people were coming back to dig out their homes. "No one wants to deal with that shit if they don't have to. In the end it's all about numbers, right? How many lunches did they feed today, that's what matters. Same reason we rescue dogs from Uptown."

A few nights ago, one of the other teams caught shit for taking a police officer's rottie while he was on shift. Nico says that it is the owner's responsibility to make sure we don't take their pet. She says if there isn't a note on the door telling us otherwise, it's fair game to break into the home. Stevie and I are trying to be careful though. We're sticking to yards. If they're in a yard, there's always a chance that they might have broken free to roam.

"Holy fucking shit," Stevie says and he throws the truck into reverse. "You see what I see?"

I don't see anything, but Stevie's got a nose for it. He jumps out and walks over to a yard with a little picket fence around it. It's early still. We're just finishing our coffee, and haven't even pretended to head out yet into the zone. There, under a bush, is a female black lab nursing seven pups.

"You in?" Stevie asks. "You ready for a day's vacation?"

I can hear a TV coming from inside the house.

***

We're driving back across town with the dog and her pups. It's total chaos, because even though we have all these crates in the back, for some reason we decided to just let them come up in the cab with us. None of us knows how to make sense of this. The lab just wants to settle under the seat and keep nursing, but there isn't really an under the seat to get to, so she's getting pretty frantic. I'm taking the pups up, one in each hand, squeezing them like produce or something, trying to pick which is best. Next thing I know Stevie hits the brakes and we are all flat against the windshield.

"What the fuck?" I say, checking to make sure I haven't squeezed the puppies too hard that were in my hands.

"I set a trap under that house," he says, pointing to a pink shotgun next to another house that is leaning like some kind of surreal work of art.

"When?" I haven't seen him set a trap the entire time I've been with him.

"I don't even remember," he says. It's the first time I can remember him seeming to care. He opens the gate along the sidewalk and runs down the narrow path between the homes. I'm still just thinking how funny it is that there's a gate there, now, after everything else that's been done. Stevie bends over and looks into the space beneath the house. "Shit," he says, and I look too. There's a cat curled up in the trap and it smells pretty bad.

Stevie pulls the trap out from under the house and shakes it. The cat rattles out stiff onto the ground.

"Why'd you do that?" I ask, as we head back to the truck.

"The trap," he says and he shuts the gate behind us.

Right, I think. If we don't bring the trap back there'll be hell to pay.

Puppies are like gold here. They slap those pictures up on the web and the donations pour in. And they don't cost a dime— we can ship those out into homes, no problem.

Everyone has their favorites. Everyone has their name on a dog or two, so when they leave town, they can take a part of the experience home with them. Nico's cooing over the mother dog; the videographer is capturing it all. "These are the forgotten victims," she says, holding up one of the pups in her hands. Once she's done I lean over the mother dog and tell Nico, "If no one claims her, this one is mine."

But for today, Stevie and I are eating like kings.

HIGH GROUND
Kris Lackey

Double respirator, steel-shank boots, prybar, black hazmat gloves, a snappy Petzl headlamp. The whole spelunker's kit hardly made a dent in the FEMA debit card. A girl named Cy at the Red Cross trailer in Arlington, Texas, gave me the card. If the feds audit me, they will approve my purchases, which will glow with sensible need. I bought the tools industrious people must have to overcome their epic misfortune.

That was mid-September, just two weeks after the storm. The Guard would wave me and my trusty Tercel through soon after that because Chez Arnholtz sits proudly on high ground. The Esplanade Ridge. No spelunking necessary at *my* house. Yes, I studied flood maps online in Rochester before I set foot in New Orleans, three years before Katrina. The maps spoke plainly. Ten minutes, they prophesied everything. When the creative writing smallwigs at Fortier University granted me admission to their M.F.A. poetry program, I Googled crime stats, income and age demographics, elevation maps, real estate prices.

"Faubourg St. John," I said to my uncle Deitmar, indicating a printed satellite photo. He unfolded his Costco reading specs, leaned over, and stared at the bent finger of Esplanade Avenue emerging from the Vieux Carre's palm and touching Bayou St. John. "Those big houses on the bayou?" I tapped them. "They were built in the eighteenth century."

"Really. You say real estate is appreciating fast? Why?"

"It's old, it's beautiful, it's above sea level. Yuppie enclave. Gay dink households. A Victorian shotgun duplex—they say "double" in New Orleans—rents for eight hundred each side."

"That's not much these days."

"Here's what one sells for."

His eyes widened. "Termites?"

"New bait and trap system. They bury cylinders around the house. It's cheap and failsafe."

He nodded. "You have a property in mind?" I took his elbow and led him to my laptop. He gazed at a filigreed Victorian duplex, freshly painted in powder blue with teal details on the spindles and dingbats. "You've done your homework." He smiled and pinched my ear. He made an offer the next day and bought the place a week later.

I kept the owner's tenant and moved into his side the week before classes began. Six months after Katrina I called Uncle Dietmar to tell him his investment had doubled. "Good," he said.

Did Professor Stapleton do his homework? As if. Fifteen years before I persuaded Uncle Dietmar to buy Chez Arnholtz, Stapleton purchased a 1950's ranch house on a slab in the Legion Oaks subdivision. You may have seen its gables on CNN. His slab rested four feet below sea level and eight feet below that mighty fucking surge that took out the London Avenue Canal Lego levee.

Stapleton had almost enough brains to get a Ph.D. from a flyover-state school. His tight-ass plainsman ethic took him the rest of the way. Ten to one the readers of his comprehensive exams were relieved when they could save their young drinking pal—and their consciences—with the word "competent." He's the type who would read assignments three times, write out and memorize responses to hypothetical exam questions, and dog-ear a hundred *Reader's Guide to* ____ books.

Legion Oaks. Sounds like a place in California, looked like a suburb of Wichita. Tickled Stapleton's nostalgia bone. Tracts of squat rancheros bricked and mortared and faux-shuttered, multiplying like invasive species, spreading like fucking melanoma into the ancient bogs of the Mississippi Delta. They were built for suckers like Stapleton. Family men who wanted safe quiet streets, a garage full of leaf blowers, Lawn Boys, and Weedeaters. A scrubbed replica of Arlington, Texas. Did he read books about this place? Did he get why generations crowded into the Quarter and Uptown and onto the ridges to escape the malarial swamps? Oh, those places had no yards, no place for the offspring to kick a soccer ball or snag grounders. Drunks and gangstas prowled the streets. Nasty hip-hop rattled the windows and drowned out little Timmie's and Sandra's Raffie CD's. Beer bottles smashed against the barred screen doors. The high ground was too low down for Dr. Nahum Stapleton and his spawn.

October 12 opened Legion Oaks for "look and leave"—a week-long window when homeowners could visit their ruined properties during the day only. Stapleton, or I didn't know him, would arrive early on the 12th. If he came with his wife, the lovely and petite Laura, they might suit up and salvage the entire week. In that case, busting with optimism, they would be towing a U-Haul trailer behind the family Odyssey. I hoped not.

The Guard and what was left of the NOPD would be swarming Legion Oaks for look and leave. My Tercel wouldn't push any buttons, but my William Blake tats and gold studs and

Jim Morrison do—the law would bend me over a Hummer in a heartbeat. My bud Jane cut my hair, and she gave me one of her Uptown lawyer-daddy's Oxford shirts to hide the tats. I yanked the studs and shaved off my imperial. A bartender friend on Magazine Street knew somebody who knew somebody who made fake ID's. I bought one with Stapleton's address and one with a Legion Oaks address on Cartier, a cross-street of Park—the second a crapshoot but good odds because it was mostly a geezer hood and geezers would be flushed or dead. The sad tale was easy—my parents had evacuated to Little Rock, I had come to search the house, blah, blah. By the morning of October 12th I was fixed to loiter unmolested. Most important, Stapleton would not recognize me.

OK. He gave reading quizzes in a graduate course. Niggling short-answer questions on those old-maid Transcendentalists. Here's a sample: "Name the three subcategories of Beauty in Emerson's *Nature*." Some doddering old queen-son-of-a-sodbuster asked him the same question twenty years ago. I mean, the Transcendentalists. Reebok quotes 'em to push sneakers. "Be yourself." Must have sounded pretty sexy to young Stapleton, hitched to a team of Baptist mules. Don't be a Baptist like your Ma, Be Yourself!

These M.F.A. programs—you can't just write, as in F.A.. They're in the academic credentialing business. They're like those ag gloms that jam cattle into feedlot wallows and stuff them with chemicals. Most people who get the card never write again. They've filled enough blue books about Emerson for the card—enough to get them through the doors of jucos and university adjunct-mills. Then they can go manqué, nurse the wound, get drunk, dream of their lost futures as free-range beef.

Stapleton doesn't disappoint. The green Odyssey creeps down Park Street at nine a.m. on October 12, sans U-Haul. I should have known he would network, learn from others the word-of-mouth wisdom: "Bring a shoebox." I am happy he listened. From my car, parked on Cartier, I can see Laura shaking her head slowly, weeping. Then she points to one ghost house and grabs her soulmate's arm. He stops the van and leans to look around her. They have seen the red brick rancher halved by a water oak, the Guard's spray-painted orange X with unit and date followed by the grim abbreviation: "1 D 0 L."

They nose into their drive, barred by a thigh-thick water oak limb. The van hums a long time as they survey the homestead, done in— all the windows sealed with plywood Stapleton precisely fitted to cheat the wrong element. He measured and cut those boards years ago, you know he did, and stacked them under his bed. Neat fake white shutters, the ranchie's failure to adapt, crusted with dun silt— all its plains armor, from brick to soffit, smeared with Pontchartrain mud. The house looks abandoned decades ago. A thousand gray oak tufts carpet the roof and dead lawn. Undulating landscape beds, Jesus they invested all the weekends of their empty-nested what-else-to-do middle age shoring and coddling azaleas camellias boxwood bird of paradise day lilies and shite knows what else. All post-apocalypse dead and dun. The sweet stench of mold, like exhaled bourbon, stains this bright autumn day.

An NOPD cruiser a half dozen blocks down Cartier creeps this way. The fake ID address turns out to be perfect—a ranchie on Cartier with a ripped old glory on its bent standard and an empty flowerbed, old folks' home. Walk into the backyard, get out of the cop's eye. I peek through a mold-blurred window at the rotted black topsy-turvy lounge chairs and beds. Black bulls-eyes etched on the walls by tide-spun end tables and kitchen chairs.

"Flashes of brilliance but a paucity of textual analysis." Paucity. Heap big word, cow student. Flashes of brilliance. Conciliatory nod, something to say about writing he can't understand. Stapleton wouldn't know brilliance if it hit him with a fencepost. Like his beloved Nebraska Cornhuskers of the 1970's who plowed up and down the field, shunning the forward pass as immodest opportunism—flashy behavior—while they bored their foes into submission.

Verso American Gothic, Laura and Stapleton rigid before the homestead, she as thin but juicier in the can, he thicker in torso. A sledgehammer in place of the pitchfork. Stapleton strides to the front door, butts it with his shoulder a few times, then lays into it with the sledge and doesn't stop. His blows thunder over the silent hood. He's showing off for little Laura, but you have to hand it to him, his farm boy training stands him in good stead. He takes down that door in short order, flings the panels aside and tosses out a few chairs before he retreats. The cops ignore him but give me, in the back yard, the once-over before rolling on.

Stapleton and the Mrs. drift back to the van, lift its tailgate and don their hazmat attire, which is, except for their white disposable suits, the same as my own. Their comic shuffle to the house in tall green boots, elbow-length black gloves, goggles, headlamps, and double respirators—part Stooge fire brigade, part Abbott-and-Costello Mars expedition—shades into hangdog pathos. Even Laura dangles a prybar. You could almost pity them.

Their first sortie is brief, less than ten minutes. They emerge sweaty and bent, stamping their boots. Laura pinches some small object in her hazmat gloves, frowns at it and places it carefully on

70

the concrete drive. Off come respirators, headlamps, goggles, and gloves. They swab their faces and hands with disposable antiseptic wipes and guzzle bottled water. They mutter together, Stapleton puts on his goggles and gloves and takes up the prybar. He strides to the house and smashes out the windows one by one, mutilating glass and wood. Rotted curtains snatch his gyrating prybar, and he peevishly yanks out turbans and unwinds them against the brick façade. The mold-rank house, bottled for a month, must breathe and dry before they can excavate familial treasure. They did not imagine slick floors, knots of maggots, soggy waist-high drifts of rugs and books, a beached refrigerator seeping pus.

When he has vented the house, Stapleton joins Laura in examining the object she has carried from the house. She rubs it on her shirt, and it glints in the sun. A watch, a ring, an old silver dollar, a child's school medal. They sense their luck and for a time turn their backs on all they have lost. Laura suddenly makes a fist over it, raises her arm and pumps the air victoriously. Stapleton purses his lips and nods. She pockets the object, they gear up and disappear into the house for a long time.

"You have not demonstrated the originality of your thesis by distinguishing it from antecedent critical analyses." I plead fucking guilty. Happy to. Proud to. What sane twenty-first-century hominid wastes a week of his short life reading loser pedant thoughts on James Fenimore Cooper's *The Prairie*? A little dignidad, leftenant, please. Ten pages of F.C.'s ass-dribble sent me to *Masterplots*, which thank you Jesus cuts to the chase. I gathered that F.C. is all chase and wrote about that very fact. Stapleton noted that this had been done before. Duh. "You are re-inventing the wheel." He, of course, was pushing nanotechnology to the edge. When the bloody Germans inspired the

American academy to rehearse and then build on prior research, you think they had James Fenimore Cooper in mind? Mendel, maybe. But not the "Adamic posture of Natty Bumppo." Wouldn't old Natty himself spin on his Pawnee scaffold and kick his stuffed dog?

It is one of those bright, hot October days—arid by local standards, stifling to the rest of the world. Stapleton and his wife burst out their front door like pursued spies. They are soaked, itchy with fear. They bear oozing amorphous cargo, which falls to the slab porch as they rip off their respirators, drink deep of the spore-thick air. When they recover, after walking in circles, hands on hips, they take up their plunder. Photo albums, I can see even from here—brown leatherette with fake imprinted gold accents. The binders disintegrate in their hands, and they are left grabbing plastic panes. Blotted, psychedelic Timmie blowing out his two candles, Sandra receiving her chemistry medal at high school graduation. Aw.

I am in luck. They scoop their plunder into contractor bags, which they toss into the van, then strip off their white hazmat suits, now scored with mold, and lay them on the curb for a FEMA crew. Thin, crooked shadows from the remaining trees fall across them and their dead lawn. It is 3:10 p.m. They pause briefly to scan the block but don't look back at their house. They drive away fast.

For the crime of neglecting the critical heritage of a nineteenth-century hack who sat in his Paris hotel and wrote a fraudulent tale about the Sioux and Pawnee, Stapleton gave me a C. This mark alone would not have ruined me. You see, I fell for all those writer tabloid photos of palm-shaded courtyards captioned with romantic blurbs from Faulkner and Hearn— all confected by Fortier's flacks—and the names of some writers I had admired, never thinking to check out the writers who actually taught there. Sons and daughters of cracker Pentecostals, Scandinavian Lutherans and other plodding moralizers. How they got a purchase in this wild den of papist fatalism, God knows.

They hectored my tales with sour hortation. "Your protagonist's motivation lacks moral consistency." "Attend to the logic of your plot." Jaysus, I didn't come to New Orleans to be lectured by Henry Ward Beecher. And my fellow students? They dutifully endowed their protagonists with virtuous sensibilities, tweaked their plotlines to syllogistic perfection. Come the dawn at Molly's, bold on Red Stripe, they went Mistah Kurtz on the faculty.

A Guard Hummer whips around the corner and bounces over the curb into my front yard. Four burr-headed teenagers in desert camo—two black and two white—tumble out brandishing M-16s. They kick open the side gate and stand in a semi-circle around me. "What's your business here, sir?"

"That's my parents' home across the street." I nod at Stapleton's house. "Can I get my license out of my pocket?"

A tall lipless acne-scarred white youth says "Yeah." He looks it over, checks the numbers on Stapleton's house, hands it back. "Why aren't you over there?"

"I was. Just looking in on the Soulagnets' house, here. Old neighbors."

"OK. Be safe." The Guardsmen shuffle back to the Hummer and roar away.

Autumn shadows spread and deepen over Park Street. The lookers have left, the Guard has left, the cops have left. And no birds sing. A starving collie, burr-matted and dazed, lopes down Cartier. You have to admire the dogs. They negotiate the rubble with headlong purpose.

73

Stapleton has opened many doors for me. And his floor plan I know from a party he hosted two years ago. The hot arid afternoon has given way to a chilly evening, so respirator and gloves don't mire in sweat. The Petzl's blue light, even aided by the sunlight slanting though smashed windows, works feebly over Stapleton's detritus. His study is knee-deep in slimy books, and because the prize is near, I fall three times en route to his closet.

He might keep his dirty secrets in his desk. But his desk, I see, has no lock, and he reared children here. No, he would raise his sin aloft and lock it tight, like a good Calvinist.

Aha. The pitiful beige K-Mart file box, in my Petzl lamp the color of a plump artery, rests untouched on the highest shelf of Stapleton's closet. And its key is in the lock, which means he trusted his wifey-poo to keep her hands off. I nudge it off its perch with a gloved finger and catch it like a football. Oozy tomes give way underfoot, and I fall backward, clutching the box. It pops open, its lock and key one rusty mass on the lid. A quire of pulpy beaver zines glops out on my respirator and smears my goggles. The sundown curfew approaches, so I should shove the porno back into the box and mine it at home, but I am trembling with buck fever. I stumble through the upended couches and broken crockery onto the patio, snap off respirator and goggles, and go to work on the contents. Each issue of *Hot Sex* or *Barely Legal* is a damp rag. The pages can't be separated, so I grasp the spines between thumb and forefinger and feel for something else. When I feel nothing, I easily rip them in two. One, two, eight, thirteen. Oh, Jesus, don't let him be a faithful husband. Make him true to form.

When I pinch the last magazine from the lockbox, an issue of *Triple X*, there is something stiff under a staple. The sun has set, and the Petzl's batteries are low. When I peel the soaked mass apart, I find a perfectly focused, un-blotted Polaroid photograph of a thin young woman I know well from many classes—Sophia Daigle. She stands naked with her back to the camera, her face and dazzling smile turned over her shoulder full into the lens. Important auburn hair drenches her back. She has written, on the back of the photo, "Stape, See my beautiful mind. XOXO, Sophia."

Section 8 is paying $1800 for half a double. Post-K I raised my tenant's rent from $800 to $1500. She didn't blink an eye. When the S-8 people occupy my half, I'll be independently wealthy for two years at least. I can sell for a third of a million, now or later. "No water" fetches big. Stapleton and little Laura will be holed up in some crappy Bucktown complex for years to come—if he isn't sacked. I scanned Sophia's lithe form and handwritten endorsement, posted them to the department e-mail list under a bogus Yahoo! name. Couldn't resist a caption: "Professor Stapleton, Fortier's American Romanticist, demonstrates his command of the field."

Nature winnows fools. Stapleton didn't heed his own plains Jesus, who said long before Darwin that the foolish man builds his house upon the sand. And some old prophet long before Jesus said that God hates a man who deals treacherously with the wife of his youth. We know perfectly well you don't have to plumb the good book for these pearls. They lurk still in zines and cyberspace, awaiting swine.

Under The Belljar
Patty Friedmann

People always remember my screen name. Belljar01. It
was good after the storm when everyone was scattered without
electronic memories, and the only way to be found was by frantic
web postings—or by e-mail sent up to the memorable ones.
That's probably how that Mariah kept track of me. I met her in
January, and I made a point of telling her my screen name so she'd
know I wasn't a simple aborigine. I worried she was down here
looking at us as some kind of hapless civilization who couldn't
explain ourselves. The night I met her she asked me if I knew the
Transylvanian. Andrei Codrescu wasn't a native, running around in
feathers, but he sure wasn't a Transylvanian.

I'm Belljar because I had Sylvia Plath's room when I was a
junior at Smith. The third-floor single in Haven House, guaranteed
to make anyone slightly mad. I'm glad to explain that to anyone
who asks, and they always ask because they want me to know they
suspect me of being suicidal. It's my way of telling them that, yes,
I'm pretty chronically depressed, but also that I got away from New
Orleans once or twice. My official biography, well, unofficial but
the one I give out, says I've lived my whole life in New Orleans
except for slight interruptions for education and natural disasters.
I was pretty much dragged kicking and screaming out of town
for both. Nobody knows I went to college kicking and screaming
because I smiled at the airport and got Massachusetts and its smells
deep into my memory. But I've told everybody that I did not want

to be hauled off to Texas after Katrina. I stayed in my house for two weeks and only left because my brother had gone to the trouble to send in a friend with a truck to remind me that I had no food and no way to get any. Wading through four feet of water wasn't worth the large number of supermarkets in Texas. I came back as soon as a grocery opened in Jefferson Parish. Electricity or not, I'm sixth-generation here. And maybe thoroughly traumatized, because we all are. But that would have been no reason for Mariah to have been down here studying me and the rest of us at arm's length and having someone pay for her to do so.

Mariah was at the reopening of the bookshop on Pirates Alley, and she looked so sincere. No one else seemed sincere, least of all me. I was there because I was asked to read. I wasn't celebrating. I frankly didn't care about anything happening in the French Quarter. The French Quarter wasn't New Orleans. I read a poem, and no one paid attention. It was about Mr. Williams the snowball man on Plum Street. Kids in the '60s figured he smuggled drugs. The poem wasn't what they wanted. A writer named Roy got up and talked about walking around the Quarter with a poodle, and everyone was rich and happy and full of whoops. Mariah seemed baffled, so I assumed she understood everything. I caught her eye, something I hadn't known to do when I was reading, and I caught her eye again when a writer whose name I didn't know read a preposterous little scene of New Orleans under water like ancient Alexandria. No one listened. Rich people don't have time for phonies; I'll give them credit for that. I thought Mariah was catching my eye because she enjoyed the silence even more than she scoffed at the story. I walked out with her, told her yes, everybody knows the man with the Romanian accent, learned within the half block to her parked bike that she was here from North Carolina, and invited her to my house. No, she said, but she would meet me for coffee. In the Quarter. I offered to give her a ride if she wanted to visit me one day.

She wasn't venturing past the lights, she told me. But there are no lights in the daytime, I said. We both know where they are, she said. I laughed. I knew what she meant. I challenged myself sometimes back then. Hollygrove, for instance, looked inhabited during the day. The double shotgun houses were intact. There were a normal number of cars parked on the streets. But if I drove through at night, the only lights were my headlights. No other vehicle passed, no house had a single bulb burning. No barrooms were open. For all I knew, electricity had been restored. But the people weren't there. And the cars didn't run. I pretended I was a child, though capable of driving, of course, and I scared myself silly. But I couldn't speed. I'd tear the holy hell out of my wheels. I took my fun where I found it. I still didn't have cable television back.

Mariah met me at the CC's in the lower end of the Quarter. I do love the Quarter, I just don't consider it New Orleans. Nobody black lives in the Quarter, except a few gays, a few bourgie types, and worst of all, a few bourgie gay types. Though at the time almost nobody black lived anywhere in the city. Nobody who was born here lives in the Quarter. (Except maybe Lindy Boggs and the woman who owns Arnaud's.) The Quarter's on high ground: that's why it's so *old*. And that's why it's so *intact*. I didn't want to patronize the Quarter. I didn't want Mariah coming to New Orleans and telling anybody that she'd seen New Orleans because she'd seen only the Quarter.

"Tell me about yourself," I said, which of course was my way of saying that at some point I wanted to hold forth on my own story. I already knew a little about her from having ordered. Mariah was skinny under her fine-knit sweater, with terrific pipe-stem arms, and she didn't think twice about ordering a large mocha with whole milk, not a word of Italian jargon, and a slab of carrot cake. She plunked down a ten for her food, not even considering the possibility of niceties. I pegged her right away as having no ability to sit still. I liked that.

"I'm here on assignment," she said.

Not that it mattered, but I didn't believe her. She didn't seem that spectacular. New Orleans was oozing words. To be paid to be here, she would have to have been spectacular. She read me. "Well, it's on spec," she said. "But I'm not finding anything ordinary. I'm practically guaranteed a story."

I looked around. We were in a coffee shop drinking what we wanted and at four other tables people were working on laptops. At the CC's Uptown, people were sitting on the pavement working on laptops. That was it. The shop uptown was closed, but the wi-fi inside was thrumming away. Maybe somebody outside might be drinking a Diet Coke, but that was it. On the pavement. "This is ordinary," I said, waving my hand around.

She had seen a second line, she told me, stepped into the moving crowd, caught a rhythm she didn't know she had. She had taken her car down to the Lower Nine, seen that barge that breached the levee, in person, herself, just like on television, tracked the rush of the water in her mind. I gave her a questioning look. It was past the lights, she admitted, but she had done it the second day in town, and it was her reason for not venturing beyond the sliver by the river anymore. She felt too hyperbolic out there.

"I like you," I said. I thought maybe she was going to take her time writing about New Orleans. Taking her time gave her the possibility of digging down to the spirit of the place. She would have to find a way not to mention food and music and water if she wanted to get it right, and for that she was going to have to take time. Since she looked like she had a sense of humor, I was willing to give her a chance. Really, all New Orleans has that no other city has is a sense of humor. I asked her if she had seen those funny T-shirts.

"Make levees, not war?" she said.

"Those are all right," I said. By all right I meant acceptable. Not funny the way I needed funny. "I was thinking of the ones that say, 'I survived Katrina, and all I got was this lousy T-shirt and a plasma TV and a Cadillac Escalade.'"

She hesitated. "Looters?" I nodded. She smiled.

"Though the Cadillac Escalade part was the police."

She pulled out a notebook.

"It's an old story. Don't even bother with it. A policeman evacuated in a Cadillac he liberated from the dealership. It's old enough to be a joke. That's the way this whole thing has to be. Old enough to be a frigging joke."

She said she would come to my house when she came past the lights. It took her a few months. Her e-mail was breathless. "I saw a fire!" She had seen a helicopter with an 800-gallon bucket drop water on a downtown fire and had pedaled madly on her bicycle toward it, and before she knew it she was out in all the neighborhoods all the time. Fire was all it had taken. She could have learned all she needed to know about the city by touring the burned-out hulls and stopping to talk, getting invited in, it seemed to me. I'd watched the horizon as the two mansions on Carrollton went up and burned to the ground the week after the storm when even the fire station was under four feet of water. Behind them lay Hollygrove. No need for disaster tours, just fire tours, a special way to see the city. The helplessness behind the helplessness. The firemen couldn't do their job. We were leaking millions of gallons of water every day in broken pipes under ground. We were oozing rich metaphors. She could have a story full of irony. Fire, not water. But all Mariah needed was that one fire. For her it was excitement. She was ready to roam the streets.

"Your house is adorable," Mariah said, looking into my living room, and I said, "Okay." I had half a house, sliced horizontally. A raised cottage, its unfinished basement had been gutted long-distance from Houston where I sat glassy-eyed, money mailed to honest Hondurans, all my memories set on the curb. The upstairs was the same as it had been before the storm, but it was freezing. I had water in the gas line. I needed a very strong male to open the pipe and empty the drip leg, I told her. I thought that was funny, even though I'd been in four layers of clothing for two days, waiting for a shift in the weather or my nephew or Entergy or, rarest or rarities, a plumber. "Write it down," I said. "Drip leg! I get maybe half a cupful of water in this section of pipe, and my heat shuts off. But it sounds like something connected to a prostate, don't you think? Nobody outside of here knows about drip legs!"

She was standing at the threshold of my house. She didn't want to come in. She had a car. I guessed I couldn't blame her for not wanting to sit and be cold, but there was nowhere to have coffee

anywhere near where I live. Nothing had reopened. I suggested PJ's
out in Metairie. They were open four hours a day. I had learned
these things. PJ's was near my psychiatrist's office. My psychiatrist
was losing her mind. She was one of only 22 in the whole city,
and she could have seen four people an hour, 24 hours a day, and
still have turned patients away. The entire metropolitan region was
insane. That was a good story. I could show her office to Mariah.
Mariah could see Northline. "I don't know about Metairie," she
said. I told her she should. But she was here to write about New
Orleans.

"Can we walk around and talk to people on the streets?" she
said. She liked being out in Treme, where she might get called
white bitch, or she might sit on a stoop and drink beer and feel like a
native.

In the past, the only people I'd ever seen out on the streets
in Old Metairie were joggers, and the security patrol probably
knew them by name and address. Since Northline got its extremely
democratic hosing from the flood, I hadn't seen one person outdoors
except construction crews. Those houses had a maximum of a
quarter-million in insurance, but their owners easily went into their
pockets for the two million in repairs. I wanted Mariah to see how
fair Katrina was.

We sat in PJ's, and she said, "I'll definitely write about this."

"Helicopters took people off of roofs on Northline," I said.
I knew a couple personally. I knew they went to the airport and lay
for three days on the floor before flying to Dallas. I didn't mention
that they found a quite fine three-bedroom apartment. That didn't
matter. The husband was still in the hospital. In Dallas. He wasn't
getting over the heat. I figured he was going to die. Probably before

he got back to New Orleans. And not to his house. I'd shown Mariah his house. It was surrounded by dead foliage. Everything was dead on Northline. Money didn't buy Northline into Oz. I'd tried out the Kansas line on her. She hadn't written it down, but I figured it was so good she'd remember it.

I saw Mariah surprisingly often in the months after that. I say surprisingly because my way of being a regular New Orleans person who saw a psychiatrist was to stay home. But my friend Sarah's way was to run around taking photographs. Sarah had lost everything in the storm, house, car, cat, everything. She had gotten on a plane to Atlanta two days before, the way one kind of sane person would have, had left a week's worth of food for her cat the way one kind of sane person would have. She put all her art, all her studio supplies, on high shelves. Covered it all with plastic. Again, she was a sane person. Maybe we would get six inches of water. Maybe her roof wouldn't hold. She'd be back on Wednesday. Now Sarah was constructively sane, living in a studio apartment with a digital camera and four changes of clothes, a laptop from which she sent me every photo so they'd all float in cyberspace, no commitments. Certainly she had no landline. "I can carry my entire life onto a plane; I don't even need to check it," she would say to anyone she met, and she met a lot of people when she took photographs. I thought she was an enviable kind of sane. So I went out with her to try to catch the contagion of motion. We were close to Sarah's gutted house on a Tuesday afternoon in April when we saw Mariah shouting to a man working a backhoe with all his might, trying to move one tree trunk from the middle of a block to the end of that block. He seemed terribly interested in failing.

I invited Mariah in to see Sarah's house. "It's not gutted to the studs," I said. Sarah had saved as many of her own artistic touches as she could. The ceramic backsplash was still in its place where the kitchen had been. Stained glass windows hadn't blown out in the bathroom. The fireplace stood free with most of her hand-painted tiles holding their pattern. It was possibly the most personal house I knew in the city before the storm. I'd sometimes asked Sarah what would happen when she left the house, and it was unspoken and wicked that I was asking about her being carried out as an old, dead woman.

"I don't go inside," Mariah said.

"Hey, I don't pay liability insurance for my health," Sarah said.

I looked at Mariah to see whether she would write that down. She didn't have her notebook out, so I figured she'd remember it. "She has to keep up her homeowner's, too," I said. "And her flood. Can you imagine?" Mariah looked bored. "What," I said.

"Oh, you know," she said. "I want to make this about New Orleans. You know, the interesting part."

I didn't say anything.

Mariah looked apologetic. Sarah was level-headed. She just waited.

"Look, I'm sorry," Mariah said. "I have to have vivid images, that's all. If I talk about insurance policies, I'll put people to sleep."

"So come on inside the house," I said.

"I never go inside," Mariah said. "I told myself when I started that it's really all on the street."

I told her Sarah now can fit everything she owns into an overhead compartment on a plane. "Think about it," I said. "We really could fit the entire city into the Convention Center now—with everything we have." Sarah started to laugh. It was a terrific laugh, such a good laugh, in fact, that Mariah laughed, too.

After that day I got several e-mails from Mariah, and though they could have come from anywhere, they came from New Orleans. She stayed and stayed and never published her story. I pictured her standing in front of a conveyor belt, old story facts falling off one edge as new ones came along. All those early months here were wasted, but it seemed to me that she would be hard-pressed to find anything to say. New Orleans was all about insurance now. Everybody was indoors. But I was happy because New Orleans was funny as hell in the saddest way. The mayor was under his bed and the congressman who was re-elected handily was being indicted for what his real self would have called pure-D greed. We were fools. Hilarious, even if only to ourselves. But none of it was in the streets, none of it had to do with food or music or water. Still, Mariah found a lot of fried seafood and warm beer, obscure local bands who told her they were famous. She helped some Episcopalians gut a house, she told me, and she imagined what it was like to drown in that house. "I went inside," she said. "And now I'm just completely ruined. But those were people I couldn't tell no."

The last e-mail I got from her was in late summer. A tropical storm named Ernesto looked as if it was heading this way. It never crossed my mind to leave town. I had told my brother that I would evacuate if anything like a slow category 2 or a fast 3 came this way, and Ernesto showed no signs that I even needed batteries for my flashlight. But Mariah wrote me from North Carolina. "I guess I've been around voodoo too long," she wrote. "I took it as a sign that my time there was over."

"I see the irony hasn't worn off of you," I wrote her back. I didn't say that I hadn't seen any on her up to that moment. "Sustain it as you write. For everyone in New Orleans, it's all I ask." I didn't expect her to write. I'd seen over time enough of her clothes. If she was writing on spec, the person who was speculating that she was going to write something was a loving daddy.

It was a year after I met Mariah, and months after I'd forgotten about her, that Sarah called me to say she'd sold the photo. *Hodge's* Magazine was giving her the cover for the July issue and paying her more than she'd ever made for any piece of art. She was mystified by their choice, an old photo by post-Katrina standards, one dating to about two months after the storm. "I'm past that; isn't everyone past that?" she said. It showed the mountain of debris on the neutral ground at West End. At the time it had seemed as if all the people who once lived in Lakeview had all their possessions in that mound. It wasn't an aesthetic photograph. Not even in an abstract expressionist kind of way. Sarah had taken it as a snapshot, she had been the first to admit. "Someone's rehashing some very old stuff," she said. We went to dinner on the strength of her check.

That someone was Mariah. I found out when Sarah got her advance copy, and she only showed it to me because she figured I'd see it eventually. She was wrong in that I don't read *Hodge's,* but right because eventually three people had no problem calling and telling me they knew I was BJ.

We are not even as evolved as aborigines. We are animals in the wild that Mariah has studied, and she has given us names to show she has been able to distinguish us from one another. Gorilla from gorilla, elephant from elephant. BJ, the Romanian, Reefer, Prep. Having sorted us out so cleverly, she was sure she also had figured out everything she needed to know about us in the first four months she was here. As I read, I saw that her chronology didn't even give us the grace to have recovered a full year. She could use so much more drama by extrapolating from the big three—food, music, water—and telling all her stories about fire, gunshots, alcohol, and strange rituals. Never once did she have to step into anyone's home. A bar, yes. A church, all right. But never a home, even if it was possible to see daylight through it all the way, front to back. "I've seen fire, I've seen rain, I've seen sunny days that I thought would never end," she quoted, to get the reader singing.

Her preference was to think she was stepping inside people. And she stepped inside me.

"New Orleans is rebuilding its bricks and mortar. But some of its people who have withstood the test of time did not wash away, and they're still standing in the ruins. Take BJ for instance. She is under psychiatric care. There are only 22 psychiatrists in the region practicing, so she must be an extreme case, but possibly emblematic of why New Orleans may never recover. I am no diagnostician, but I would guess she is manic-depressive. Her e-mail screen name is synonymous with "suicide." Yet for her everything about Katrina is a joke. She won't talk about the storm unless it's a joke. She can't take it seriously. She has to laugh.

"BJ's everything that is wrong with New Orleans. Manic-depression is my diagnosis for the city. How can they have Mardi Gras and Jazzfest when half the population is in exile?

"BJ will tell you upon first meeting that she is a sixth-generation New Orleanian. With people who cling so desperately to the past, New Orleans will never face the future."

I don't think I want to see my psychiatrist anymore.

THE ESCAPE
Berman Black

When Dickie didn't show up for work Monday, Mike called Dickie's sister first and then Dickie's mother.

"They got him downtown again, Mr. Mike," she said. "You can call after him if you want, but he'd probably rather sit there."

The two brothers, Mike and Doug, stood in front of Doug's house. Doug's box truck was loaded up with materials. We were starting a new job that day and there was a lot of work to do. Doug smoked a drug store cigar with one foot on his running board. He was over six foot and lean, with scars all over his hands and feathered grey hair combed away from his face. He looked exactly like a man who had been working hard at plumbing his whole life.

"We need to call down there and get Dickie," said Doug as he waved to one of his neighbors in the driveway across the street. A cat appeared from beneath the fence, meowed and brushed its face against Doug's jeans. He bent over to pet it.

"I told Dickie not to feed this thing," he said. He shot me a look. I was sitting on the stoop reading, my lunch between my feet. "You feed it now."

Mike took out his clipboard and reviewed it. At close to two hundred and fifty pounds, Mike was nothing like his older brother Doug. He had big thick arms and a big neck, a dark moustache and fat round feet squeezed into a pair of running sneakers turned black from grease and dirt.

"I got Dickie and you scheduled for all day," Mike said to his brother. "So you better take the new one and get started. If I can get Dickie out, we all can jump on the job tomorrow and make up the day."

I'd been with them close to a year, since I got into town, but I'd always be the new guy. I put my head in my book and tried to relax until it was time to start working.

Doug tapped me on the shoulder.

"You can also be putting up the tools in the van while we sort this out," he said before grinding the cherry of the cigar on his boot heel and walking past me back into the air conditioning.

Orleans didn't have Dickie, so Mike called Jefferson on the off chance he'd been picked up there. They'd didn't have anyone by that name at JP either. It was past nine. The morning rain had come and gone and the sun was out heating up the sidewalks and streets, making it hard to breath.

In Doug's van, every tool had its own place. Rows of bins and shelves with fittings and parts that chattered as we drove down the streets. I was arranging the tools in the back when Mike came out and sat on the bumper. He lit a cigarette and made a call on his cell phone.

"They said they don't have a Dickie, Ms. Brown," he said.

"Well, you might try asking for Daymond Brown," she said. "Or sometimes he uses Donald."

The next day I was arranging the tools and sweeping the van, waiting for the brothers to finish up inside, when Dickie came walking up the street, his boots untied. He had his Walkman in one hand and a cup of coffee in the other.

Dickie was maybe forty with a mouth full of silver that made it hard to understand what he was saying if you'd just met him. He had big forearms snaked full of veins and a dirty baseball cap with NO printed on it that Doug had bought for him a few weeks back at a gas station on Claiborne Avenue. Dickie sat down on the bumper and sang along with his music under his breath.

Mike came out with his clipboard and pulled the head phones from Dickie's ears.

"You sure a hard one to find, Dickie,' said Mike. "But not for the cops, huh?"

"No," said Dickie.

The cat came when it heard Dickie's voice. It rubbed its face against his leg. Dickie dug in his pocket and gave the cat some pellets.

"You don't got to pay us back for the bail," said Mike reaching down to pet the cat. "You can come out on Saturday and wash the vans. That'll make us even."

"I was fine where I was," said Dickie. "Another day and they'd of let me out."

"See how grateful?" Mike said, giving me a kick with his dirty sneaker.

"I see," I said.

"Am I right, huh?" he gave me another kick. I put my head deeper in my book. "Tell me I'm right."

"You right."

A week later, Dickie didn't show up in the morning and Doug said to forget about it because we had too much work to worry about where Dickie had gone this time. Mike went to catch repair calls and I rode with Doug, on the side streets snaking from Jefferson into the city, tools flying off the shelves in the back.

The house we were working on that day was a raised double off Earhart. On the other corner, there was a big job started. The workers had cleared a lot four doubles long. The HVAC guy working in the double next door to ours told us the Catholics were building six new modular homes on the site. The lot was mud, turned black from trash and gasoline, busted water lines maybe under the dirt. Throughout the neighborhood the streets were tore up. In front of the house we were working on, the sidewalk was in chunks from where yellow excavators had been working.

"Clear this all out," Doug said to me, "And get started by finding the water meter."

The year before I left Flagstaff, Arizona, we had a homemade bowl out in the woods for skateboarding when we didn't feel like skating in town. An above ground swimming pool, shaped like a keyhole, and built from stolen lumber. The deck had been built around a tree for support. It was always being skated when the sun was up through a spring, summer, and a fall, but in winter it snowed, hitting four feet deep in the shallow end. We only hiked out there twice that winter. Both times, we climbed into the snow and shoveled out the bowl. When we reached the layer of ice beneath we poured gasoline all over it. The fire melted the ice and dried out the masonite. Then we skated for hours. Laughing, boards flying out of the bowl and diving into the snow.

In New Orleans, the heat inside the cab of the van mixed with the cigar smoke. I got in the back to collect the probing rod and the sharpshooter, two regular shovels, Dickie's big orange screwdriver that he liked to use for digging, some old gloves from the crate, and the hose to wash off the tools before they went back into their spot in the van. I put the screwdriver in my back pocket and got to work, the spade of the shovel weighed down by the caking mud, digging in the sun.

AFTER THE MUSES PARADE
Amanda Anderson

That first week, I did not dream. Each night I passed out, dead. Each morning, I awoke shocked. First the flooding. Then the looting. And the fires. Finally, the snipers, firing at the rescue copters. Each day unimaginably worse. Yet every morning, Barry shook me awake with the latest news, as if my knowing would help somehow.

So much action, and we stayed frozen. Sitting on his momma's sofa, we drank mojitos with mint fresh from her garden. We watched well-groomed reporters talk of "the tragedy, the unprecedented tragedy," as mint leaves swirled in our glasses, dancing with the ice cubes. Our drinks: the only thing left alive. Barry's momma bitched at us for watching too much TV; it was making us sick, she said. Get out and exercise, she said. Here's passes to my gym. So Barry got up and fixed her leaky window, and I went online to search for clues of what happened to our house.

It didn't look good. A couple blocks away from us, the grandstand at the Fair Grounds lost part of its roof and was flooding fast. The WWL website predicted nine feet of water across the city. Everything was fucked. I could see the water rising up to my paintings, the moisture wicking through their canvases. I'd never framed them, not that a frame would stop the water. Once the canvases soaked through, the mold would create its own diseased patterns over the faces and buildings I'd so painfully rendered.

I drank a few more mojitos, then put an ad up on Craigslist: "Lakeside property for rent. Well-appointed, with artist's studio. Cheap!"

When we'd left New Orleans on that empty Sunday, I made sure to bring my Buddha statue and my sixty-day chip. I'm not very religious, but I needed strength. I needed assurance that things would be okay. Mostly, I needed to breathe without gasping. As Barry drove past boarded-up buildings, I tried to focus on my breath, my fingers working the chip. I considered the Buddha and the impermanence of all things, how our world is really a dream. On the radio, some fucker warned anyone staying that they'd better have an axe to hack through their roof. I flipped the radio off. Barry reached over to play with my hair, singing with a lilt: *Oh my Sadie, my brown-haired lady/ Who witched me with her smile/ She's my curly girl, a whirly girl/ Stay with me for awhile*…

Three hours later, I still couldn't breathe. When we stopped for gas, I crossed my fingers and bought the last warm beer.

Two months later, we drove home, but first I spent over three hours in the Lafayette Wal-Mart. What would we need to survive? I grabbed mosquito coils and rat traps, beef jerky and peanut butter. I wheeled three full shopping carts to our van. Barry surveyed the cases of beer and bottles of booze, the boxes of crackers and the mountain of toilet paper. He turned to me, his doe brown eyes as soft as his voice: "Sadie. You forgot batteries."

We took back roads to get home, and out by LaPlace we began to see homemade poster-board signs adorned with crosses and hearts: "Bless You New Orleans," and "God Be With You." Instead of comforting me, the signs made me nervous: things must be bad if the swamp folks were praying for us city heathens. Real bad.

It sounds made-up, but I swear it started to stink as soon as we crossed into Orleans Parish. Jefferson Parish smelled fine, but we passed that parish sign on Earhart and suddenly the car filled with the rotten funk of death, of acrid, stinking life abandoned. If I were to paint the smell, I'd use olive-greens and black-browns, with streaks of baby-vomit yellow.

Thanks to my long shopping trip, the sun was setting as we crept into the trash-filled New Orleans streets. Instead of people, ruined refrigerators gathered on corners as if waiting for the bus. Caved-in walls and blasted-out fences, felled trees and miles of trash, downed power lines and mangled street signs: all of these whispered a sad welcome. Halfway through a bottle of gin, and I'd never been so sober in all my life.

We pulled up to our house and looked at each other, me and Barry. Even though we'd had the place for five years, it was still a dump. Barry's the kind of guy to start sanding a wall, prepping it for paint, then suddenly stop and decide to build a deck. It used to drive me nuts, but I made up my mind to rise above it and finish every painting I started, to prove a point. This bright idea of mine is what brought me to AA in the first place. I told myself that if I could just finish one piece, I wouldn't have to go, but six months later, I had a pile of half-painted canvasses. So I sucked it up and went to my first meeting.

If it hadn't been getting dark, we might have sat in that van for hours. Barry let out a long exhale: "OK," he finally said.

I followed him to the wooden side gate. The doorknob was rusted over so bad that Barry had to WD-40 it to get it to turn. Then we had to clear out all the fallen branches before we could get the gate open. I knew our live oak would make it through the storm – she's a good twelve feet around – but I didn't think she'd be so stripped down. About half her branches were lying at our feet.

By the time we cleared a path through the courtyard for Barry to get inside, I could see the stars between the few branches left on our tree. I stood there in the dark, thinking that without electricity, New Orleans was just like the country, with only the bugs and my own thoughts to keep me company.

A little while later, Barry emerged. His hands shook as he lit a cigarette, and I was glad the dark covered his face. After several drags, he spoke. "Let's sleep in the van tonight," he said.

I guess I should be grateful that our place was such a wreck; if it had been fixed up nice, seeing it after the flooding would have done me in. I'd braced myself for the mold and the water lines, but I hadn't realized that even the heaviest furniture, like my granny's armoire, would float in the floodwater and end up wherever it liked. That piece had collapsed on top of the TV, which lay face-down on the dried mud, as if shielding its giant glass eye from seeing the wreckage. A few outfits still hung in the armoire, mud-stained and trapped on their hangers. Barry's Shop-Vac, which we kept in our living room, had drifted into the kitchen and hung itself from the ceiling fan.

Some folks might credit God's mercy for the drought we had after the storm, giving us a rest from the flooding, but I personally feel as if He wanted to get one more laugh at our expense. The mud covering our floors had cracked from being so dry, so when we clomped through with armloads of shit for the curb, dust rose up in clouds. There we were, trying to clean that storm out of our lives, while we huffed dried particles of flood sludge. I tried wearing a mask, but with no rain, it was hotter than ever, so having that mask on felt a little like I was torching my own face. No power meant no air conditioning, no fans, and no ice. None of us should have been surprised that folks stuck here during the storm went crazy; with a giant pond of flood water to humidify that heat, it's a damn miracle everyone didn't just kill each other.

So you will excuse the overused metaphor, but Barry and I were literally in hell. We slaved all day in the ruined moonscape of our home, wearing sweat-soaked clothes and heavy boots. Barry got to eulogizing everything he carried, to the tune of "The Old Gray Mare": *Our old TV she ain't what she used to be/Ain't what she used to be/Ain't what she used to be/Now it's full of mud.* Because the house was so nasty, we slept in our van every night, which began to smell like a locker room, that is, a locker room where people regularly smoke cigarettes and spill beer. Of course, if it weren't for all the beer, and my ability to drink it warm, I surely would have stabbed somebody.

And that's how I came up with the idea to burn everything we owned. We were already in hell, may as well get our fire and brimstone on. Besides, I got sick of looking at my ruined paintings sitting on the trash heap that no one was coming for. It was like watching a baby bleeding in front of a silent audience. My neighbors walked around the heap to bitch at me about their troubles, and it took all I had not to shove their faces into the molded, stinky shadows of my world before the storm and moan with despair. My portrait of Sailor Sam, posed on top of the Andrew Jackson statue ready to fly out like a bird. My boys from Joe's Cozy Corner, cutting up on their barstools. Little Big Man, playing a trombone with a slide as long as he was high. All of them, now pockmarked with mold and attracting flies. Oh, no. It was time to destroy our lives with a little respect.

Barry wasn't as keen on the idea. "You know what kinda stink that's gonna make?" he asked.

"You know what kinda stink we got?" I asked him. "This whole demoralizing situation calls for a bit of dignity. For fuck's sake, they burn the goddamn flag just for touching the ground, and I think our lives are a little more precious than that piece of cloth."

Barry ran a hand through his graying hair. "Leave the flag out of it," he snapped. "If you want to torch everything, by all means." He stormed into the shed and flung a gas can onto the ground between us. "Look," he said, "it's even got gas in it. Must be a sign." He turned and went to the van.

"You're leaving?" I shouted as he pulled away. He didn't answer me, just stared ahead grimly as he clutched the wheel.

I popped open another beer. Nothing like marriage to make you feel completely alone. It was just like him to run off when I had a big job to do. Never mind all the help I gave him on his goofball projects – digging a koi pond in his momma's yard or selling umbrella hats outside Jazz Fest – sometimes, marriage is just a losing deal. Not to mention the fact that before the storm, I couldn't wipe my ass without some itinerant wanting to help out for a few dollars, and now that I really needed a hand, there wasn't a soul to help me.

I take that back: as I dragged my first load of trash back from the curb, Mr. Leonard from next door hobbled up.

"Hey pretty miss," he said, leaning on his cane. "You decide to keep that trash?"

"No, Mr. Leonard. I'm burning it."

"*Burning* it? Where?"

"In the courtyard. The ground's dead anyways."

"Well, now. You don't think the neighbors will mind? Drought like this, that fire'll spread."

"I'll be careful. You know, I was a Girl Scout."

"Girl scout? What they know about fires?"

I sighed. "Mr. Leonard. Are you planning to help me with this trash?"

"Look at me, girl, I can't drag trash!" For effect, he leaned forward on his cane.

"Then I'll be getting back to work now."

Mr. Leonard had stayed through the storm, had sat up on the second floor with his Ermetta, a cream-colored Pomeranian weighing all of fifteen pounds. If the rescuers took dogs, he might've gone, but Mr. Leonard wasn't going nowhere without little Ermie. And thank God for that. He's the one who chased the looters away from our house; if he and his old rifle hadn't decided to stick around, no telling what we would have come home to.

So Mr. Leonard and Ermetta sat on their stoop and watched me drag trash for the rest of the day. He offered helpful commentary along the lines of "Don't you burn that plastic, now," and "That fire department already got too much to do." Ermetta panted in the afternoon heat, head pressed against the cement as if the world were crushing her neck; at least the dog empathized with me.

When I couldn't carry any more trash bags, I went ahead and lit the fire in an old clawfoot bathtub Barry had planned to turn into an outdoor soaking tub. I doused my paintings with gasoline and tossed three matches: for the past, for the present, for the future. The canvases blackened and withdrew into themselves, twisting and warping, as if my subjects' souls really had been captured in the paint, and the fire was now wrenching them free. I couldn't watch, and yet I had to watch.

I was pretty far gone by that point. I could hear words in the crackling of the fire, which reminded me of Buddha sitting by the river, how he could hear all the world's stories in its gurgling. Unlike the Buddha, though, when I bent over to make out the words, a lock of my hair caught fire. I swatted it out, laughing: it's not a good drunk until someone gets burnt.

Wherever the hell Barry went, he better bring more beer home.

I tended to that fire for weeks, during which time I got to chat with everyone within smelling distance, including boys from the National Guard and folks off the Red Cross truck. I should have guessed that the smell of fire would attract people, as we'd all become sensitive to impending disaster. But the fire stayed in the tub, its porcelain forever blackened with the ashes of our lives. No one seemed that surprised that a drunken lady like me would set her life on fire; in fact, Caroline and Maia, the older lesbian couple around the corner, burned clumps of their moldy paperwork as they argued about whether or not to stay in New Orleans. At least Barry and I didn't need to have that fight; all our money was tied up in the house, and we had nowhere else to go, except back to his momma's place in Lafayette – which was not an option.

Any ideas I had of experiencing some sort of restorative, Buddha-like epiphany at the fire went up in a black smoke that smelled of burnt plastic. Instead, for the first time in my life, I became the most popular girl on the block. The Red Cross stopped by every day at 12:30 to drop off lunch, and my neighbors, procrastinating on their own homes, showed up to eat spaghetti out of Styrofoam and drink water from aluminum cans. Everyone needed to talk, and if people in New Orleans were open about their personal lives before, now they'd turned inside-out: spewing their most personal details into the world and keeping niceties like *hello* and *how are you?* to themselves. Mr. Leonard, as an eighty-year old man with commando storm tales, was a big hit, as was Lyle, Miss Evelyn's daughter's boyfriend, who'd been at the Superdome for four days. "No one can tell you what really went down, unless you was there," Lyle told us, and I believed him.

In a perverse way, our little fireside chats reminded me of AA meetings, except that we drank warm beer instead of coffee. We were consumed with our own life troubles, and had to admit that we weren't in charge, but merely puppets dangling from the hands of a "higher power." (With an emphasis on "higher." As Lyle said, "What kinda crack God been smokin' to cause this shit?)

Ironically, now that I wasn't going to AA meetings anymore, I finally would have had something to say. I never could understand how all those sober people could be so close. Their little club, jacked on coffee and fiend-smoking cigarettes, yellow-toothed and repentant, confounded me. If you could be part of a club without drinking, then why the fuck would you need AA in the first place?

I did call my sponsor Sheila right after the storm, just to let her know that I was alive. Thank God I got her voice mail. I left a slurred message that I wasn't dead, just stuck in Lafayette. She called me back the next day, but I didn't answer. Her voice message implored me to stay strong and keep working the steps, but I didn't call her back. She left a few more messages saying the exact same thing, and finally quit calling.

That was it: I needed a Katrina sponsor. Someone to steer me in the right direction, to help me with FEMA and the insurance, someone to assure me that I wasn't throwing my life down the shitter by staying in New Orleans. Instead, I had Lyle, and Mr. Leonard, and Caroline and Maia, none of whom agreed on anything. Maia, with her wrinkled suntan and faded batiks, was hell-bent on moving to New Mexico, and wanted to let the city bulldoze their place. Over her wire-rimmed glasses, Caroline argued that they should milk the government for as much as they could to redo their house and rent it out before they left, not that she wanted to leave. Mr. Leonard, leopard-print scarf circling his straw gambler hat, said they were both silly girls, and that no one would be getting money from anyone. Lyle, after smoking a joint behind our tree, would wander over to the fire and start talking about the Superdome.

It's possible that Lyle may have been bending the truth some, but to hear about the apocalyptic conditions in the Dome made our own sad stories seem a little brighter. So you lost all your possessions? At least you didn't have to shit in front of hundreds of people. Your old auntie died? At least you didn't have to carry her stiff corpse through the mobs just to find a spot to dump her.

Because of Lyle's vivid stories, I began to dream again, dreams where the five of us wandered around the Superdome, empty except for piles of corpses. In one dream, I peeked out of the Dome and stood frozen as a giant wave – hundreds of feet in the air – threatened to crash down on me. I woke up with a start, the sleeping bag under me slick with my sweat.

Once in awhile, Barry would join our little group for a beer or two, but then he went back to work measuring walls and drawing up plans. He coped with the damage by plotting a better house, and I could hear him in there, singing about camelbacking off the kitchen and putting in some "grand old stairs." If I was going to listen to bullshit, I'd rather it came from the neighbors and didn't involve a musical ode to an imaginary dream home.

To keep the fire going, I had to venture farther and farther away from the house to find shit to burn. With our wheelbarrow, flood-stained with dark water lines, I wandered around the neighborhood looking through the trash. I mostly looked for wood, either lumber torn from ruined homes or broken furniture, but I discovered all sorts of treasures in those piles.

If I'd realized that people had been throwing out perfectly good stuff, I would have left that fire weeks ago and gone trash-digging. A lot of it hadn't been touched by the water: I scored designer purses and Tommy shirts, brand-new shoes and piles of books. Lots of baskets. There were bags of Mardi Gras beads, of course, but I found a stash of vintage glass beads, which I brought home and hung from the remaining branches of our oak tree.

Orange and gold, green and blue, purple and pink, refracting the sunlight into flashes of color: it was like Mardi Gras all over again.

Before long, I'd abandoned the wheelbarrow for the van so I could bring home tables and chairs, old-time gas heaters and even an old porcelain stove. True, the bigger stuff had been in the floodwater, but with a little elbow grease, most of the flood scum came off. I brought Lyle with me to help lift, which made things more interesting. When I'd been on my own, homeowners either ignored me or brought things to my attention: *this bucket might make a cute planter*, or *hey, did you see these shelves?* With a black man at my side, you can imagine the looks we got: dirty, dirty. We came home filthy from the looks. A couple people chased us off. One man went so far as to ask if Lyle was bothering me.

"Oh, no, sir," I purred back at him. "He's my house nigger. He drives me around."

We then walked to the van, and Lyle made a point to get in on the passenger side. He glared out the window as I drove off. "Find somebody else to do this shit," he said.

"I know," I said, staring straight ahead.

I'd hoped that Barry would become my new trash buddy, as he'd been excited that I finally left that stupid fire. Plus, he loved junk as much as I did, which was good, as my flood finds were taking over the yard.

But when I asked him over our morning coffee to come out with me, he begged off: "I'm working on our house, babe." He got up and grabbed a hammer. "Or do you want to sleep in the van forever?"

"Just this one time," I pleaded. "There's this great mosaic-topped table over on St. Peter. It'd be perfect for my studio."

"Your studio?" Barry asked. "Have you *seen* your studio? It needs a lot more than a table."

"I know, I just want to grab it before someone else does," I said, taking the hammer from him. "After we get it, I'll help you with the sheetrock."

Barry sighed and pulled his keys from his pocket. "Just this one time," he said.

Someone had obviously put a lot of love into that table on St. Peter. The entire top was covered with tiles of all colors – midnight blues and mint greens, lemon yellows and silvery-plums. A string of candy-red tiles twisted through the center, forming a path through the riot of color. That path was what got me – I'd even dreamt about it the night before. I was belly-down, moving along the path like a snake. I began to feel wet, and looked down to see my front covered in red. It wasn't blood, but tasted more like Jell-O. Then I woke up, thirsty for soda.

Even if I hadn't had that blood/sugar dream, I needed that table. When we got there, Barry agreed that it was a sweet find. He hopped up into the van to pull it inside, while I stayed on the ground to push it in towards him. And then, wouldn't you know it, my old AA sponsor Sheila jogged by.

"Sadie!" she shouted. "Oh my God!" She held out her arms to hug me, but then realized that we were moving a table. "Let me help!"

Admittedly, it was good to have her there, taking some of the weight of the table as we lifted it up to Barry. After we got it in, she gave me a hug.

"How are you, sweetie? I've been thinking a lot about you."

How was I? Suddenly glad that I resisted pouring whiskey into my coffee that morning, that's how I was. "Great, Sheila. Really great!"

"I haven't seen you around," she said, and by "around," she meant at the meetings.

"No, we've been real busy on our house," I pointed to Barry. "My husband, Barry."

"We got six feet," I continued. "It's been a nightmare, but fortunately Barry can do most everything himself."

Sheila looked at me, and I knew she thought I was full of shit. Which I mostly am. "Self-reliant," she said.

"Oh, yeah. Barry's the best." I stepped toward him, and he rolled his eyes at me.

"And you, too," she said. "Being on your own."

"Sure, of course," I said. "Just putting the pieces back together."

Sheila nodded. "Well, if you need anything," her voice trailed off. "Do you still have my number?"

"It's in my phone," I said, lifting my phone up to suggest that I might actually call.

"Okay, then," she said. "Good to meet you Barry. Sadie, don't be a stranger," she said, patting my shoulder.

"I won't," I called out as she jogged away.

Driving the table home, Barry asked me who Sheila was. Another annoying thing about AA - that veil of secrecy, not being able to introduce people as who they really are.

"She was my sponsor," I told him.

"Oh."

I knew what was coming.

"You ever think about going back to meetings?" Barry asked me.

"No, I do not."

"They might help you feel better," he said, glancing over at me.

"I feel fine."

"You might be able to paint again," he suggested.

"I don't think my painting is a priority right now. We need to get our lives back."

"And collecting junk is getting our lives back?" He pulled to the curb and stopped the van.

"What are you doing?"

"Sadie," he said, turning to face me. "I'm living with Fred Sanford here. You bring crap home all day long and then pass out every night."

"So you're not getting any, that's what this is about?"

He scratched his head until his hair stood on end. "This is about you, that's what it's about. You are one marriage away from becoming a bag lady."

"Well, thank God we're married, then. So you can rescue me from the streets."

"Sadie. I know you're not happy. It's okay to admit it."

Something in his voice made me tear up. He was always so kind.

"I'll be fine." I gasped, trying not to cry. "I just really hate those meetings."

"I know you do," Barry said, gathering me to his chest as I began to sob. "I know you do."

***

Self-reliance: it was the only way things got done in our broken city. Street signs blown down? Residents painted their own and nailed them to posts. Entergy still hasn't come? Generators roared across the city. No FEMA trailer? Folks commuted from Baton Rouge. You're an alcoholic who wants nothing to do with AA? You rebuild your life with your own two hands.

At first, I worked with Barry putting up new walls. I should say, Barry worked and I stood around, holding sheetrock in place. Arms sore, brain dead. Barry sang near-constantly, and when he got stuck on a punk riff – *sheetrockin', oh sheetrockin'/ buildin' walls just to tear em down* – for the better part of an hour - *sheetrockin', oh sheetrockin'* – I went to work in the courtyard.

New Orleans had finally turned the corner into fall, and the air felt crisp as I bagged up the brown, brittle remnants of our once-lush yard. The brackish floodwater had choked everything except for the elephant ears and our live oak. Animal or vegetable, catastrophe proves us all to be either heroes or pussies.

Stuffing ruined plant matter into plastic bags is just the sort of menial job that inspired me to be an artist – never long before I'm compelled to blow it off and start drawing. For the hundredth time, I considered painting again, but why? Who wants to look at a series of black panels, or a study in gray with brown waterlines? More importantly, who wants to paint it? I'd seen the shutterbugs out in the streets, everywhere, framing shots of the devastation – surreal at any angle – and thought, *Ah, yes, now everyone's an artist. The muses float amongst the ruins.* But those bitches would have nothing to do with me.

I had no yard, I had no ideas, but I did have my junk. I wandered over to my mosaic table and walked my fingers over the smooth ceramic. If I hung the rust-flaked mirror on the fence right behind it, I had twice as much table. Not bad. Next to the mirror, I hung a cross I'd found, which I'd only taken for the black Jesus hanging on its wood. Even if He was missing most of His legs, I never could resist a black Jesus.

He needed some mourners, so I rummaged through and found some pink kewpie dolls that I'd rescued from a trash pile. People had come from all over the country to save the abandoned dogs and cats and turtles and parakeets, and even a few folks arrived to help the people in need of rescue, but who would save the muddy Barbies and the war-torn Santas and the model horses from the wreckage? No doubt the ruined toys were the most depressing aspect of the storm, as hardly any children remained to play with them, to clean them off and give them new homes. It was up to me, and Lyle, until the blatant racism forced him out.

Lyle had had a thing for rubber duckies – don't ask me why – and so I lined them up behind the others at the feet – um, I mean the waist – of Christ. Then I set up my Buddha statue on a pedestal made from a paint can covered with cloth. In my yard, the Christian and the Buddhist toys would worship together. I would have incorporated more religions, but I didn't have the props.

It was a touching little scene, there under the oak tree and her glass beads, so I decided to turn the yard into a church of the black, legless Jesus, where the Buddha meditated at His side. But first I donned one of the several construction helmets I now owned, and marked the front with a black cross: now I was really ready to work.

By the time Barry came out for a cigarette, I'd gotten most of the junk arranged. The toys now sat on rows of chairs facing the mosaic-table altar, flanked by tables covered with baskets of plastic flowers. I even had an offering dish: a Frisbee filled with doubloons. I was on my knees, scooping ashes out of the clawfoot tub when Barry surveyed the scene and shouted, "Sadie! What are you doing?"

"Cleaning out the baptismal font," I replied.

He gestured to a trash bag, half-full with dead plants. "I thought you were working in the flower beds."

"I thought I was too," I said, standing up. "But I needed to do something with all this junk." I pointed to the altar. "Pretty cool, huh?"

"What *is* this?"

"Think of it as a sanctuary," I said, walking over to him. "When you're feeling overwhelmed, you can come here and get some peace from the Buddha or pray to my black Jesus."

Barry squinted over at Him. "Is Jesus missing his legs?" he asked.

"He gave those legs for your sins," I replied. "Although they probably just broke off during the flood."

Silently Barry took in the whole scene for another minute. "It's creepy," he finally said.

"Churches can be like that," I replied, squeezing his hand. "But I'll take it apart tomorrow."

And so it went. Buzzing with nervous energy that I used to dampen with beer, I spent long hours rearranging my junk. To justify my demented playing, I took photographs of each "installation" for slides to send to galleries. Another side effect of the storm: the whole city became intoxicated by a sense of historic importance. What gallery would be able to resist art made from the lives of genuine flood victims? With this in mind, I became more creative on my junk forays, expanding beyond stuff that could still be used, to broken tennis rackets and smashed guitars, stained clothing and mattress springs. When I found a pile of mannequins outside a shuttered store, I nearly wept with joy and brought them right home to stage a murder scene.

I invited Mr. Leonard over one day to see the 20-foot tower that I built from junk. He never goes anywhere, so I thought he'd get a kick out of my junk sculpture. But I was wrong. "Girl, you need a job," he spat at me. "Thank God you didn't break your neck on that thing."

Evenings were the hardest. Around four in the afternoon, my energy slumped and I'd want to revive myself with a cocktail, but the specter of AA loomed large. If I gave in and started drinking again, I knew I'd have to go back. So I took long hikes around the city, returning home in the twilight hour when the fading light accentuated the brown waterline that had strangled us.

We bought a new TV to have something to do at night, since I wasn't going anywhere near any bars. TV is a shitty drug replacement, like trying to soothe a heroin addiction with table sugar. But it hypnotized me long enough, from dinnertime until bed, when I'd take my FEMA-administered Ambien, and lose consciousness. When I stopped drinking again, I'd hoped to have brilliant dreams like I used to, but the sleeping pills cut me off entirely: sleep was simply deep, and completely dark.

At least we'd finally moved out of the van, and on an air mattress in our old bedroom. We'd begun to eat normal meals again, not just hot dogs roasted over my trash fire. With the electricity back, we could keep food in the fridge, and even if we couldn't use our gas stove, we could eat salads and make stir-fry in an electric griddle. Of course, now that I'd stopped drinking, I had to get my cheap sugar from ice cream and candy and Hubig's Pies. My sweet tooth was out of control, but I indulged my new sugar habit as a reward for staying sober.

You can't live in New Orleans for long without realizing at some point that Mardi Gras is coming and nothing you can do will stop it. There was some brief talk of canceling Mardi Gras, out of respect for the dead and displaced, but the city couldn't stop it, either. So I planned to ride Mardi Gras out at home, stay away from the parades where everyone and their granny all drank together in Carnival camaraderie. I wouldn't last five minutes out there. Instead I stayed home and sewed costumes for the mannequins. I vowed to celebrate Mardi Gras in a new, sober way: by stitching ball gowns from scraps of discarded clothing. The literal fabric of the city, pieced together by hand. (I had yet to find a working sewing machine in the wreckage.)

So I missed Krewe du Vieux, and the first weekend parades, and even the doggie parade in the French Quarter. But no surprise, it was junk that brought me back. I'd read in the paper that the Muses would be throwing plush spears instead of the plastic kind: a Mardi Gras first. As I sat sewing old T-shirts to each other in hopes of making a magical gown, I thought, *what the fuck.* Like I said, the sense of history had thickened the air, making every little thing a

116

Significant Event. The first post-Katrina Mardi Gras was sure to be legendary, and who was I to miss it? Besides, I wanted one of those spears.

I'd bring a thermos of coffee with me and have Barry at my side, to keep me from temptation. And again, another crucial moment in our marriage and what happens? Barry deserted me. Granted, his cold did seem pretty miserable. Ashen-faced and sweaty, he croaked out a low, nasally ballad – *my muse leaving me/ don't you go, don't you go...* Still, in our early years, he would have whiskeyed up like a champ and come out anyway. So I left for the parade alone, with only my thermos and my good intentions to keep me sober.

Never mind that I'd intentionally arrived at the parade just as the Muses were rolling, so I wouldn't have to stand around like an idiot bored and waiting. And never mind that I found a spot away from all the bars, where I wouldn't run into any of my old friends. Forget about my coffee and the chocolate-covered peanuts in my pocket.

Forget all that, and remember rolling spotlights shining through confetti. Stiltwalkers on their tiny shoes. Revelers flashing sashes and marching bands, strutting together in perfect formation. Music blasting from their horns and vibrating from their drums, booming deep within me. And remember ladies rolling past, in satin costumes trimmed with gold, sitting atop sparkling floats forged on Mt. Olympus, floating bubbles and screaming neon. "Muses Got Game," the secret theme revealed, where each float showed a game with a post-Katrina twist: refrigerator hurling and barrel of monkeys, contractor wrangling and the blame game.

117

Remember all these glories, for they explain why no one stays sober for long. When one of the college guys standing nearby offered me a beer, I had it to my lips before I could tell myself no. With so much magic outside, why not pour some of it inside?

Suddenly I was painting again, if only in my head. I'd do a whole series on the parade, glowing blue-green under the streetlights, against the black night beyond. The giant shoe made of pink light. Ebony girls in glittery suits, waving pom-poms. Horse teeth, flashing white. The royal capes of violet and the sassy orange tunics. Red-striped marchers and brassy golden tubas. The crowd, covered in beads of every color, their hands reaching up to the dark heavens.

Why was I using junk to rebuild a city of such color? Did I really think that sewing mold-stained clothes would help anybody? What had sobriety done to me?

The very last float had no riders, only a large goddess head lit from below with orange light, as if from the fires of Hell itself. A tear clung to her giant cheek. Mnemosyne, the mother of muses and the goddess of memory, rode alone to remind us of the departed ones – those drowned and carried off, those moved to safer ground, and those dead from heartbreak.

As the goddess rolled by, I lifted my soft spear in salute. I thought of the Buddha, who teaches us not to get too close to this world, and my black Jesus, who got too close and lost his legs. Still. Someone had to paint the survivors, and someone had to paint the ghosts. And how would I know them? They would find me in my dreams.

STRAY
Jennifer A. Kuchta

A stranger would attribute the broiling, bi-polar madness to living in the aftermath. To post-traumatic stress. To returning to a house still standing in a virtually abandoned post-Katrina New Orleans. But Meredith's screaming, her wide-eyed insanity, is the same old, same old. The same old bullshit dished out in the same old digs, just under new terms and conditions. Meredith is the one thing in all of New Orleans, from the east to the west, from the lake to the river, that is, on this early October day, exactly the fucking same as it was six weeks ago.

You stare across the sweltering kitchen at her waiting for this most recent rampage to end, taking relief in knowing that even with the windows open wide to air out the house, no one will hear her scream. A million coffin flies flit around the kitchen, in and out of the sink, in and out of your nose and eyes.

"Why don't you want chicken?" she yells, her chest heaving from her near hysterics. "Tell me, Lisa! Why don't you want chicken?"

The space where the refrigerator once stood is empty except for the plastic gallon jugs and cases of water stacked there. The new one won't come for another week, and the old one stands at the curb like a shining, silver tombstone. Every day since your return, you've had to walk to the A&P up the street. When it's open, it closes at three, so if you want something cold or fresh, you pray for ice. The first day you went, they had ice. There wasn't any the

121

next two. But the real problem isn't the lack of ice, really, you don't mind eating out of cans, but how that store smells. Even cleaned, the store still reeks of rancid meat and milk and bleach – a triptych of smells that put you off thirty-six years of meat and dairy.

"I've already told you, Meredith," you say calmly, brushing the flies away from your face. "I just can't do it. Not meat. Not yet."

Tears are running down her face. "I want chicken."

"Then get chicken. I'll eat something else," you say, praying for a lull in what's been twenty minutes of madness.

You'd like to say you've never seen this side of your girlfriend, would like to believe that it's the heat and the flies. That it's the long silent nights save for the sounds of the military Hummers rolling in pairs down the street every few hours. That it's the lying awake trying to decipher any other noise that periodically sounds – noises you never heard in twelve years of Uptown nights until now. Or that it is the joblessness – yours on hold until January and Meredith's lost to the flood. But it's none of those things; it's been three long years of sudden outbursts that cut you to your core. And you have stood by for all of them.

Purple rings Meredith's eyes, which are cliché-ly wild and inhuman. You wish you had a camcorder to record this episode, so you could say to her later, "See? This is what you're like. This is why it hurts." Maybe that would change things.

She grabs your arms and gets up in your face. She smells of stale lettuce and spit.

"Why don't you want chicken?" she demands, digging her nails into your arms.

You jerk your arms away silently counting to ten, wanting in every ounce of your soul to retaliate, to smack the shit out of her. Make her stop screaming, and screaming, and screaming. If you had a gun, you'd put a fucking bullet in your head.

"This is ridiculous. Don't you see how stupid this is? You're screaming at me because I don't want chicken."

But she can't understand that, won't understand that – isn't fucking capable of understanding that there is no logic there. She probably doesn't even hear you. You are probably just a sweaty blob in front of her with a hole that opens and closes letting out a stream of undecipherable sounds. When the sounds end, she starts up again. You've long known there is no reasoning with her when she is like this. You just have to wait it out. It will end in one way or another.

Bigger tears pour down her face, and she turns on her heels and stomps off into the bedroom. The bed frame squeaks as she throws herself down on the bed, sobbing uncontrollably, as if someone has just done her real harm.

Except for Meredith, the house is quiet. There should be twenty other feet trampling through the house, but for now there are only eight. Those eight belong to Meredith's two cats who meowed nonstop the first three days you were back. They had survived being left behind. Like everyone else, you figured you'd be back in town long before Labor Day, that you'd kick back in Austin in a dive motel watching CNN with the dogs for a couple of days and then head on back to town. But three days stretched to five, and when New Orleans stayed sunk, you hit the road again, pulling farther and farther away from home.

Luckily, cats are like roaches, and Morris and Reed not only survived but are fatter than when you left them. It was Meredith's choice to leave them behind. You had told her she had to make the call because they were her cats and they'd have to ride in her car because your truck was already packed with one hundred and eighty pounds of dog.

The twelve missing feet belong to your three dogs still safely evacuated with your mother who will kiss their ears and rub their bellies until their hind legs flail. You left them because you didn't know what you would find when you returned. Word on the street was that your fences were down, and loose or otherwise missing dogs weren't to be risked. So you patted their heads one last time, one yellow, one orange, and one black, and drove away without them, without looking into their eyes.

Your fences are battered and bent, but they mostly still stand. At the front of the house, you had to chainsaw a fallen crepe myrtle off of the low chain-link fence surrounding the front yard. When you returned, only the portion of the tree on your property still bending the fence remained. The other half had already been removed by some invisible hand. There are broken cedar pickets at the back of the house; still, the fences would have kept the dogs safely corralled, and you miss them. But they are playing and romping with your mother and her dog through acres of Colorado wilderness, smelling after squirrels and rabbits and chasing hawks and mule deer. You won't bring them back until the end of hurricane season, until Thanksgiving, and November seems impossibly far away.

In the other room, Meredith coughs and sniffs and howls, and you realize you jettisoned wrongly.

After waiting and wading through long lines at Home Depot, you come home with enough cedar pickets to replace those snapped by sailing tree limbs and siding and old metal awnings. Meredith is in the house watching yet another hour of *Little House on the Prairie* not seeing the irony nor dichotomy between the Ingalls' situation and your own.

You hold a fresh new picket in place with your knee and hammer it in place. As you bend to nail the bottom of it to the rail, a medium-sized, rust-colored dog comes down the street, and you pause, hammer in the air. The dog sniffs at the mountain of trash and sheetrock piled in front of the house at the end of the block and then squats to pee. She's a dog you've never seen before – not loose nor in a yard nor on a leash – some sort of spaniel mix. Slowly, you lower your hammer. The dog has a hurt hind paw, and when you whistle, she stops dead and stares down the street at you.

"Come on," you say, squatting and setting down the hammer. "Come on, girl."

The dog doesn't move until you stand again, and then she jigs back up the street and up the next block. You start after her, and she jogs faster, her hurt foot flopping along beside her. By the time you get to the end of the block, she's gone.

You go back to the house to get some dog biscuits and dog food, already imagining what you will do with the dog if you catch her, how you will tame her and gain her trust. Meredith is lying on the couch with a can of Miller Lite clutched to her chest, watching as Charles plows a field.

"There's a stray," you say, heading through the living room and into the kitchen. "I've never seen her before."

You stuff a handful of multicolored bones into your pocket and fill a Styrofoam bowl with dog food. You grab an old leash and head back through the living room.

"Where are you going?" Meredith asks, looking at you over her can.

"There's a stray," you repeat slowly. "She's got a hurt foot."

She turns back to the TV. "Someone probably left her."

You nod. "I've never seen her before."

She shrugs. "People do shitty things."

One of her cats waltzes into the room, and she snaps her fingers at it. It meows silently and kneads its paws on the edges of the brand new rug, catching its claws in the nap. Meredith turns and stretches one arm out with a groan. Like her cats, she has gained weight since the hurricane.

"You want to come with me?" you ask.

The cat rubs against the back of Meredith's hand, squinting its eyes at you. "No," she says, "it's too hot."

"I'll be back."

Armed with dog bait, you head up the street in the dwindling daylight. The fading light and the ceasing of pounding roofers and speeding contractor trucks probably brought the dog out of her hiding place. And hunger, of course. New Orleans was full of strays before the storm, but in your years in this neighborhood, in this immediate area, strays haven't been common. Sure, sometimes there was a random loose dog or maybe stray, but never a real live scraggly stray like this one.

As you consider the anomaly of the stray, your mind wanders back to the horror stories told about dogs in the first days after Katrina. Dogs were left on highways and on rooftops and in boats. Dogs were left chained while the city filled with water – left in bathrooms and kitchens while houses sank. Those realities are why you don't watch the news anymore – can't and won't watch the news anymore. They say babies were raped in the Superdome and dogs were shot in a school in St. Bernard, but deep in your heart you know which one of those rumors is the absolute truth.

When you reach the big blue Victorian on the corner, you are reminded of the photos taken of dogs standing on porches looking on as their owners drove away or as news crews took their pictures but didn't or couldn't help. Pictures and videos of dogs standing in trees and clinging to fences, the strain of holding on on their faces, in their eyes, dark, oily water swirling around them. You can't see that footage anymore – not one more time, not one more image ever ever again. Tears suddenly fill your throat as you place the bowl of food next to the crumbling sheetrock and moldy couch where you saw the dog last sniff.

One night before the storm, coming back from a club in the Quarter, you paused at a stoplight on Elysian Fields, waiting to turn left and take the highway homeward. As you waited for the light to turn green, movement in the dark across the street caught your eye. There behind the Chicken Box takeaway was a skinny, skinny stray. Even in the darkness you could see her teats hanging nearly to the ground. She sniffed all around the dumpsters and back of the store, hoping to scrounge up some tidbit – chicken bones probably all she'd be lucky enough to find. And as the light turned green, you imagined razor-sharp shards slicing their way through her belly, leaving her dying a horrible death on a horrible corner while her puppies met their fate under some semi-blighted house or someone's boot. Or worse.

As you rounded the corner, she came around the side of the building and into the light. Ratty fur hung off of her, a dirty yellow. Her ribs were like burglar bars around her chest, a maybe once-green collar around her neck. She carefully stepped through the empty parking lot, her tail curved downward behind her. As you picked up speed, her head popped up and she looked right at you, pausing with a paw in the air, sniffing.

You always looked for her when you passed that corner, day or night. Some nights you'd see her, sniffing and creeping. Some nights you'd let out a gentle whistle, and she'd stop her search and perk her ears at you, looking but not trusting, trotting away into the darkness with her head half turned over her shoulder to make sure you weren't coming after her. And you didn't. The most you ever did was throw some dog bones to her. You never saw her in the daylight – not like this dog. Chicken Dog was too clever to get caught out.

Then your body starts to shake, the shaking starting first in your arms and shoulders, and then vibrating down through your chest and into your thighs. You have to sit down on the dirty sidewalk next to the trash as you are overcome with sadness. Soon you are sobbing and gasping in the silent New Orleans twilight, clutching red and green dog bones in your fists.

For a month you search your neighborhood for the dog. She lopes awkwardly down the street every now and then. Usually, you catch sight of her out of your kitchen window when you wash the dinner dishes, but by the time you get outside, she is nowhere to be found. Her coat has grown more ragged, her limp more pronounced. On one of your tailings, you followed her to a parking lot where someone had scattered some dog food. And even though the food was kind of dusty and dirty, the sight of it still made you feel better, helped you to regain some hope in humanity.

And over that month, Meredith has grown even fatter from beer and TV, always promising to help you with this and that, promising to get a job, to do something more than sit on the couch. The new refrigerator purring away has only encouraged her laziness as has the A/C rumbling away in the back yard.

But you, you have sawed and hammered and fixed. You have secured the roof as best you can so that no more rain pours through it. Tarring and hammering in the blazing hot sun, slipping on loose asbestos shingles, still waiting for the insurance man to come. In the mirror you notice that your pants sag more around your hips than they did before, that your cheeks are sunken, and that your eyes seem strange. Your skin is covered with welts and scratches and scrapes with origins you can't recall. The worst is a slash across your ribs that appeared after you nailed a piece of flashing back on the roof. You often find yourself absentmindedly rubbing your fingers over the scab marveling that whatever did the damage didn't cut through the thin skin there to your ribs.

And between searching for the dog and working on your house, you drive around town checking on friends' houses and the remains of friends' houses. You burst into tears when you come to a streetlight that is finally working for the first time since the storm. You've become the scout for those not yet returned, those wanting to know if there are gas stations and grocery stores open, if others have moved back to their blocks. You've come to hate them. You hate them for staying away and talking like they know what the city's like while you have been here over a month. Hate them for seeing October and the beginning of November someplace else: Atlanta, Seattle, San Diego. For being able to buy groceries or eat at their favorite restaurant whenever they want. Getting to watch football where the seasons change, while here there is just one: hurricane season.

This month has given you too much time to think.

Eventually, you go to look for Chicken Dog. You know she won't be there, but you can't let go of the thought of her sitting there day after day waiting for life to come back to her restaurant.

From the highway, you can see blue roof after blue roof. You can see burned out buildings and a broken and battered skyline. This is your first trip east down the I-10, and you try to remain stoic and positive about what you see and don't see. When you turn down the off ramp, your heart starts to pound, and you reach over and finger the worn blue leash, knowing full well that you won't need it. But you need to go, need to see for yourself that she isn't there. You should have looked for her sooner.

Her corner is abandoned and dirty, the restaurant empty and flooded out. The gas station across the street is the same way. Aside from the cars whooshing by above you on the highway, nothing moves. No roofers here. No trucks picking up garbage with huge mechanical pinchers. You are the only one around.

Slowly, you pull up to the restaurant and park. When you get out, the early evening heat comes down on you all at once. Looking through the cracked and filthy glass, you can see that the place hasn't been gutted yet, and you wonder why, fearing that if you dare to breathe you will smell what must be nearly three-month-old rotting chicken. You circle the building, expecting to see Chicken Dog when you turn each of the four corners, but still there is nothing. Not even a dried up yellow corpse of her.

You poke your toe at the dirty brown-gray water line on the back of the building and then turn and look across the empty lot to see that same water line on the houses lining it and on the fences next to them and running all the way around the rest of the lot. Turning still, you follow the flood line across two cars, an old Cadillac and a truck, and then across the street on the oak trees in the neutral ground. All the way across the street the water line continues marking more houses and running across the gas pumps and then the street lights and street signs and lampposts. You follow that dirty line with your eyes until you are spinning and spinning and spinning, following that water line like you used to do with the ceiling fan blades when you were a kid. You'd force yourself to keep your eyes on just one of them until you'd get so dizzy following it around and around that you'd fall down hiccupping on your mother's shag carpeting, watching the room spin.

And even though this isn't your first water line, first flood line, or the first time you've thought, "I wouldn't even be able to drive here, I'd be under water," this is the first time you laugh until tears come to your eyes. This is the first time you puke black coffee on your bare toes and on the dusty, cracked cement.

If you lie down here, you'll drown.

Later, you step through the front door, the bile still in your mouth, and Meredith rises from the couch screaming.

"Why did we come back here?"

Confused, you try to switch gears, try to catch up with her and where ever she is. "What's the matter?" you ask, pushing the door shut behind you.

"I talked to three people. Three! Why can't they just hire me on the spot? They'd be damned lucky to get someone as good as me."

"What are you talking about?"

"Three interviews, Lisa. I talked to three different people. Nobody hired me."

"But everybody's advertising."

She snorts. "I don't know what they're looking for then. Some skinny Tulane bitches that will suck their dicks?"

"But Tulane isn't even back," you try.

"I wish this whole fucking place had just been destroyed. They should just blow the whole fucking thing up and start over. It's already destroyed. They should just finish it off."

A thousand bits of reasoning flit through your head. You want to sympathize about the job thing but not when she's yelling at you.

"I thought you said we were staying in Colorado."

"I never said that."

"Why did we come back?"

"For the house. For your cats."

She pauses for a moment, and you feel the cool of the A/C wash over you. You want to sink into the couch and just collapse. To drown in coolness.

She kicks the coffee table. "We should have gotten the cats, turned around and left. I hate this fucking place. It's not my house. My name's not on the paper."

And off she goes into a tirade you've heard a thousand times before. You are tempted to finish it out yourself. That would be the better choice. Instead, more out of tiredness than anything else you say, "Then leave if you're so unhappy."

She freezes and turns on you – a gaze so filled with hate you are surprised when you don't turn straight into stone. Perseus had it easy.

"What? Are you kicking me out now? So you can bring some little bitch in here?"

You drop into the couch. "What?"

"Is that where you go, huh? You have some little bitch? I will find her, and I will kill her, Lisa. I will kill the bitch."

"All I said was leave if you're unhappy."

"Is it Marie? Huh? Is that who it is?"

If the dogs were here they would have all scattered – would have run out of the room like there was incoming enemy fire. When things calmed and quieted down, you would have found them huddled together under your desk – big dogs turned to shivering, shaking wimps. And they would have crawled out from their hiding place one by one, heads low and tails ever-so-slightly wagging, looking at you with big sad eyes and pressing their heads to your chest.

Your breath comes in rapid pants. You put your hands over your ears and squeeze your eyes shut tight, humming, but you can still hear her ranting on and on about how she "will kill her" and how "you have no right to do this" to her, about how you owe her unconditional love.

She slams through the house, up and down the hallway screaming at the top of her lungs, banging the doors and walls with her fists. You drop to your knees and crawl to the desk. As you duck beneath it, folding yourself up into the fetal position and singing gently under your breath, you can almost feel your dogs around you: Sam, and Misty and Max.

It is your fault for being here, for hitting the road the second the city opened back up. You wanted to be boots on the ground. Wanted to come back and get things moving. To get your house and life back in shape after weeks away. You were excited to come back. To be home. But save for the cats and checking on the house you didn't have to come back. It's your fault.

And you rock and rock and rock.

The house is silent. You open one eye and look out into the living room, straining your ears for any sound. Nothing. Slowly, you unfold yourself, limbs prickly and asleep, careful not to make a single sound. If you are lucky, Meredith is passed out asleep in bed and won't wake for a long time. You shake the life back into your legs, and then creep through the bathroom to peek into the bedroom. Meredith is on her back in bed dead to the world, someone on CNN chattering away on the TV.

Carefully, so carefully, you pick up your keys by the front door and pull it open, closing it more gently than ever behind you. You do the same with the gate and then tiptoe across the yard, through the chain-link fence, and out onto the sidewalk. Your truck sits waiting, the streetlights reflecting across its roof and hood. You unlock the door and start to swing it open, hoping that for once it will forego its telltale squeak. It does and you slip behind the wheel. For a long time, you sit in silence waiting for the front door to fly open. Waiting for Meredith to come screeching out onto the porch.

134

Waiting with one foot still resting on the curb so that you can say you were just getting something if Meredith does come out.

Just as you are about to finally pull the door shut, in your rearview mirror you see the orange stray gimply marching down the middle of the street. Instantly your hand finds the long blue leash still resting on the passenger seat. You slip out the open door and drop silently into the grass beside your truck, holding your breath, feeling your heart pounding in your temples. On your belly, you can just peek beneath the truck, and between the tires, you see three legs and a flopping foot slow and widen their path as the dog passes, suspicious.

When she is past, you push yourself up with Superman force, and catching both yourself and the dog off guard, you fling yourself upon the matted mess. She cries out, and you can feel her bones beneath you as your hands loop the leash around her neck.

Rocks and glass and branches bite into your elbows and knees as the dog thrashes at the other end of the leash, putting up a fierce three-legged battle, rearing up on her one hind leg and crying out as if she's being skinned alive. She falls to the blacktop and gets up again and again as you pull her towards you, shortening the leash. You wait to feel her teeth upon your skin, knowing that it will happen, and when it does, her mouth painfully on your wrist, you still don't let go. You hang on because you know that she is scared, and she is hungry, and she has never been in this situation before.

When she lets go, the two of you pause, lying in the street, panting and huffing in the hot still night. No one comes out to investigate. No porch lights flicker on. No Hummers hum by. No Meredith. You look at the dog and then slowly rise. She watches you out of the corners of her eyes as you get up and open the back

135

door of the truck. Reaching in across the back seat, you run the end of the leash through the door handle on the opposite side and start pulling on the leash, similar to an old trick you used to use to load ornery horses as a kid. She fights and bucks until she is twisted up against the running board of the truck, her front feet braced, and then she looks at you, looks into you, searching. You want to reach out to her, to pet her, but it is too soon. Instead, you give the rope one last pull, and, surprisingly, she scrambles into the truck, dragging her hindquarters in behind her.

You shut the door and fling yourself into the driver's seat, hoping she won't lunge forward and attack, won't go berserk. You turn over the engine and wait. When nothing happens, you step ever so slightly on the gas and pull away from the curb, headlights off. You take one last look over your shoulder, accelerating as you do.

REALITY IS A TRIGGER
Tara Jill Ciccarone

In the mornings before I'd go to The Lambda Center, I'd
go to group and talk about the three of them because you weren't
supposed to talk about men in AA as much as I had been doing.
Sometimes I'd talk about the way Jack and I had drank while
fighting through the toxic mess of us, or about Jules and the way
his drinking made me want to kill myself so much that he'd hit me,
or about John Carlo and that I just loved him then. Everyone was
trying to take my love for him away, calling it codependence. The
anti-depressants the clinic had me on weren't working, but I wasn't
drinking anymore. A woman in group therapy was telling me my
brain was pickled.

"That's why you want to be with this John Charles," she
said. Her T-shirt was a long-sleeved tie-dye with a picture of Daffy
Duck waterskiing, and it hid the permanent sleeve of scar tissue that
stretched from her left wrist to elbow.

"John Carlo. Like the racecar driver," I corrected. "Why
don't we talk about why you never remember anyone's name?"

I was learning a lot about manipulation, there in the
therapist's office that looked like it had been assembled from debris
from a leveled house. Brown paint peeled from water-stained walls
and the fake wood paneling was almost all but missing, giving
the impression that there was a window there in the middle of the
labyrinth that was The Chartres Mental Health Center. The whole
place was a Rorschach test with brochures that asked if you'd been

drinking too much since hurricanes Katrina and Rita taped up, as if that was news to any of us.

Melissa was her name. She couldn't go to the grocery store because the liquor aisle was a trigger for her. She had once taught ballet.

"You need to be more independent," she was telling me. "Sell your plasma. Go to the plasma bank in Metairie and sign up."

"I don't like needles," I told her.

"You never shot cocaine?" a heroin addict asked, and I shook my head. I was the only one who hadn't. There were five of us in group therapy but Melissa was always taking the group hostage. I was the only one who had a job, even if it wasn't starting for a while. I was supposed to be humbling myself and living life on life's terms and being honest about what a mess I was, but these women never believed me. My bottom didn't seem low enough for them to believe I was telling the truth.

"You remind me of myself at your age," Melissa was saying. "I was so obsessed with my high school boyfriend."

I was thirty-one, but everyone said I looked much younger, especially without any make-up on. I'd finally gotten the haircut that I'd wanted my entire life, and blond layers curled just at my shoulders. Pounds dropped off of me.

I was 29 days sober, and they all thought I was going to relapse. The doctors had me on so much Campral to cut down cravings that I never knew if it was the meds or some actual peace of mind that kept me from walking through the plastic curtain of The Abbey, the most terrible bar I had ever loved, and into a vacuum.

140

They were back on the plasma thing. Somehow, the therapist had decided this was a good idea, her approach being based on contradicting any instinct I had.

"I'd rather clean someone's house. A lady from AA wants to pay me."

"Does she have a husband?" the therapist asked me.

"I don't know if she has a husband."

"She's asking you because the husband might have alcohol in the house," Melissa explained.

"I doubt there is alcohol in the house. Anyway, the lady will be home."

"What if you relapse together?" my therapist wanted to know.

"You should really think about selling your plasma," Melissa was saying. "They don't have alcohol at the plasma clinic."

"What about rubbing alcohol? I drank that once," I lied.

"You get 40 dollars and you can sell it twice a week."

"I'm anemic. They don't want my fucking plasma. They just don't."

And this would go on and on until noon when I would run out of The Chartres Mental Health Center and go to The Lambda Center for AA.

In AA you weren't allowed to cross-talk and there was good coffee and the women would give me their phone numbers even though I never called. The noon meetings were small since the storm, so I'd have to share most of the time. I sometimes found these little crystal memories that alone made sense, but with everything else were as convoluted as the rest of my life. But the people at The Lambda Center knew me from these little crystal

141

moments, knew that I was as crazy and sad as the rest of them had once been. I could tell them I wanted to sit in bars and do cocaine even though cocaine didn't work anymore. I just didn't know how to be a wreck without it.

But there were these moments I could make sense of to myself that made me understand just how sick I was, which I interpreted as knowing there was hope for me.

Jack and I were living in Mid-City after the storm when only a gas station that sold beer in cans was open. We'd walked there past the furniture that landlords had put on the neutral ground when their tenants weren't coming back, making little living rooms all down Carrollton. The kitchens were across the street on the sidewalks, taped up refrigerators that no one knew what to do with. But that had been the day before. Now I'd been drinking all morning and afternoon. I couldn't get the heat to turn on because the gas lines had water in them. We'd been back in the city for three weeks, four weeks, our whole lives. Drinking relieved the Katrina cough enough that I forgot the black mold that was growing in my lungs.

I was shivering in my bathrobe when Jack came home, astonished that I'd drank so much and insisting that I get dressed and walk to buy some more beer. He was always making me do things I was too drunk to do like walk, or have sex, or cook some kind of food I wouldn't want to eat. But he was secretly glad I was so drunk because it gave him permission to get sloppy; it was there like a pact between us.

We had to hurry home because it was getting dark and we still had curfew then, the National Guard patrolling with their guns, and the dogs, abandoned during the storm, forming packs. The streetlights didn't work on Esplanade or Carrollton, making the Humvees one of the only light sources on the way back. Migrant workers were living in little tents on the neutral ground of Orleans Avenue in front of our rented shotgun, the night quiet save for the hum of generators and occasional Latino music.

"I don't want to carry this beer anymore." I knew I was whining. "I'm so full of beer I might crash through the earth." It was a 30 pack of Bud Light. "You should have bought some whiskey on your way home, Jack."

"You shouldn't have drunk all the beer we had," he told me.

"Will you crawl under the house and bang on the pipes?" Sometimes that made the heat work, and if the heat worked, maybe I would love him that night.

But he never did, and I never could. By the time we got home, we were fighting because I had interrupted him.

"Can you do anything but get drunk and clutter up the place?" he yelled at me as he shoved some flood damaged photographs I'd found onto the floor. I'd been collecting them from flooded out houses all over the place. It was what I did when I wasn't drinking or getting MREs from a Red Cross tent, which was another thing that annoyed Jack. I couldn't remember what he was looking for.

"Here, I'll help you," I offered, but I was tangled up in a blanket, and my legs were made of pudding.

"Just stay on that couch," he shouted.

"Maybe you should tell me what you lost again, Jack. Did you ever think of that?"

"I already told you four times."

That was when I dropped a cigarette in the couch. He was in the other room, slamming around as the cigarette burned through the cushion. I tried to pour beer into the hole and spilled it everywhere.

"Can you bring me a beer or some water?" I called. "What are you looking for?"

He was still rummaging around in the kitchen. "I'm looking for the times, you dumb bitch," he screamed. We hadn't been able to get our hands on a newspaper since we'd been back; I didn't know if they were being printed at all.

The couch was smoking, but as long as I kept it from him, it wouldn't be true. I found a half empty beer from the morning and aimed some at the hole, but it was a waste of time, not because all I had to do was tell him the couch was on fire or go get some water myself, but because we'd been pouring beer on whatever we messed up for so long everything reeked of it.

"Will you come in here?" I started to cry.

"I'm looking for the times."

"What fucking times?" Because they had been there, a long time ago, before the hurricane had been the little scrap of cotton that finally cracked us. "Don't you think I am, too?" I was gulping down air, about to sob. I pictured him the way he had been, clear-eyed in wingtips in the Quarter, drinking only a few beers with me before the vodka and the whiskey and the cocaine had come.

"I'm looking for the times for the bus. I told you the buses are running again, you dumb bitch."

"I fucking hate you, Jack. I fucking hate you so much."

I'd talk about those days sometimes in Al-Anon, that with Jack it had all started. I'd be at an Al-Anon meeting because John

144

Carlo and I wouldn't be together anymore, before we'd find one another again and make life more tolerable for a little while. But sometimes I'd mention Jack and that with him I'd believed I had no choice in the matter but to drink and didn't know if he'd felt as destined to ruin as I had or if he still hated me. But he's in an apartment in Uptown with most of my furniture and won't answer my calls, even when I call him from psych emergency, and I had only the few alcoholics at the noon meeting to answer my questions.

It was raining over The Lambda Center, and nobody could hear as a storm crashed down on the tin roof, but I knew that the person sharing was talking about being able to have one drink, but at the bottom of it there was always a pile of cocaine.

"Reality is a trigger for me," the guy next to me said.

Sometimes I would cry for the person I had been or for the men who couldn't heal me and who I couldn't save and where that kind of thinking had gotten me to begin with.

I left Jack for a drunk named Jules who promised to take care of me forever, or in reality, I slept with Jules in a blackout and never went home and said I was sorry to Jack. I'd taken up with a bunch of people who Jules was drinking with, and I ended up staying at a house on Dauphine Street that a beautiful gay alcoholic named Aaron owned. There were a bunch of them there with psychedelic mushrooms and tequila, and my coke dealer L.T. knew them too. I couldn't keep up with them, so I did as much cocaine as I could get my hands on, so Jules would love me forever. But something went wrong.

They would come to me in Aaron's backyard the next morning, and someone would tell me I needed stitches and give me more whiskey instead. It was All Saints' Day. My slut costume from the night before had blood all over it. Aaron and John Carlo were with me, drunk and up from the night like I was and sitting in a bunch of wheelchairs someone had stolen.

"Say the word," L.T. said when he showed up, but I couldn't remember why Jules, my savior and alcoholic boyfriend, had hit me over and over until somebody called the cops.

"I want mountains," I told L.T. instead.

And there they were, in glistening white piles. We all sat drinking, blowing railroad track lines like we'd all been beaten, and maybe we had. Jules had been one of us, and my shame was all of our shame as the morning blurred into afternoon.

Aaron's four enormous dogs were shitting all over the backyard. The neighbor sat in a wheelchair, off to the side, grinding up some OxyContin pills so we could snort them. John Carlo cleaned the gash above my eye with some rubbing alcohol, but nobody had any Band-Aids.

"I can't look at him the same," John Carlo said. It was he who had cleaned the blood off of me outside the old Hideout in that fried hour right before dawn. John Carlo and Jules had been kids together. I knew John Carlo had begged Jules, the only person who would speak to him, to get him out of a crack house he couldn't afford, and a few weeks later, Jules had beaten John Carlo up in his bed for buying crack with Jules in the car. That was my idea of real defeat, not being hit in a blackout, but being hit in your sleep for doing something that was killing you anyway. But John Carlo was better now; he was only blowing lines. We were all proud of him for that.

None of us were going to work. It was still the day before. We all had parts of our costumes on, an assortment of masks and wigs; Aaron was still dressed as a pimp.

I needed to get my stuff from Jules' place. I tied up my bag of powder. "I'll share if you come with me," I told John Carlo.

There are times when the smallest details can sum up what seems like the end of your life. My fishnets were torn to shreds, my cell phone in two pieces. The Virgin Mary amulet my grandmother had given me had disappeared.

"You have a black eye." John Carlo handed me his sunglasses because mine were gone.

A neighbor met me on the sidewalk, some guy I'd met once or twice. "You have blood in your hair," he said.

"Yeah, I think she knows that," John Carlo said.

"Jules doesn't remember," was his only reply. He gestured toward the apartment. More blood was all over the steps. They had let him out on his own recognizance.

"That was stupid," I told John Carlo. He followed me in.

Jules had pulled his curly hair back in a ponytail. He sat on the floor puffing on a joint. Later, Jules would tell the court that I'd fallen on a pile of tools on the floor. By then, I would have dropped the charges, believing there was some good in him. But this wasn't the day for forgiveness.

I stripped down to my bra and panties.

"You need to look at me and see what you did," I told him. I had bruises all over and some thumbprints on my neck, gouges on my inner thighs.

"Why, Jules?"

Tears streamed down his face. I didn't know who he was crying for. "I don't know," he answered in a tone I'd never heard before, as if he was the one who'd been beaten. I didn't want anything to do with that.

He was a washed up drunk, heartbroken for the soul he'd been drowning for years. I saw he had an ass-pocket of Jim Beam, and I took a swig from it. I'd eventually hate him so much that he'd leave town for a rehab in another city, believing the story about the tools. But in that room with the half-pint between us, he knew what he'd done, the way I knew only his hands could heal me from it. I wanted to kiss him.

John Carlo shoved my clothes, the only possessions I had anymore, into a garbage bag, cramming them in, and we were out of there before the coke wore off.

People came by to do it with us, and the day went on like that, the bunch of us telling the story. As long as I kept telling it, I didn't have to think about what I would do next. Aaron came back with some people he'd met at The Abbey, some gutter punks with a pit bull. The woman wore a pink wig. The guy smelled like piss.

"I just like to mind my own business until I black out," he said.

They had half a bottle of Taaka vodka and some bar coke that burned like battery acid, but I wasn't sharing my shit with them.

"You might as well sleep here," Aaron said, but no one could.

It was always like that at Aaron's. A day was really one long night, and the stories always gained momentum. Jules had choked me until I'd passed out. He'd probably raped me. We were tougher than everyone, but we were always being beaten down when we least expected it, bragging about our shame.

The next morning, I went to Verti Marte to get some cigarettes. "You look like hell," the cashier told me. I wandered into a bar on Esplanade where everyone had heard I'd gotten my jaw broken and was glad it wasn't. I had survived, and everyone bought me drinks, snorting key bumps in the bathroom and mourning my injuries and listening to the story over and over. L.T. found me there. He still wasn't taking my money. The coke was better that the last bag. "I feel like an angel just left my shoulder," I told him.

"Halloween's over," a tattooed girl who was too young to be in there said. "It's Day of the Dead." I was still wearing a corset and tutu.

"Then die," I told her.

"You should really go home," the bartender said. She'd seen all of this a hundred times, addicts becoming shadows, but someone ordered me another drink, and she poured it.

It went on like that until John Carlo came by, looking for me, or more likely, looking for more of the drugs. He helped me into his truck.

"Something happened," he said.

I offered him some whiskey.

"To Jules?"

"No. Forget Jules. I'll show you."

***

There were cages of birds all over Aaron's living room, parrots and cockatiels. "Those people from The Abbey brought them here," he whispered.

The birds were magnificent. Their cries shook the air like a box of glass. It was hard to believe there was that much beauty left in the world.

"Where is everyone?" I asked.

But John Carlo didn't know.

"I think they're stolen," he whispered to me.

There was always something new in Aaron's house. The gutter punk boyfriend had cheated on the girlfriend, and she'd brought all her birds over to get away from him, but the birds had freaked everyone out so much that they'd gone off to a bar.

I still had an eight ball.

"My hands are shaking too much," I told John Carlo.

He cut out two lines, and somehow I got it to go up my nose.

"I have my period," I told him.

"I don't care."

"Will you hold me after?"

And he did, all through the night until the sun shone ridiculously into the room, glaring into my cocaine morning.

There are moments like that, when you've been crashing for so long every door in your head has slammed shut and your skin feels like it was meant to be scratched from your body. I gripped him more tightly, his clammy arms around me.

"Do you miss Jules?" I asked.

"I miss him."

"Me too."

I didn't go back to Aaron's for a long time. I'd live in a FEMA trailer, a bed and breakfast, and a girlfriend's bed before I'd get my own apartment, but for a long time, I'd still be there at Aaron's house, jittery and wondering how it had all gone so wrong.

I talked about that morning at The Lambda Center and that John Carlo had gotten me to leave and give him my drugs for my own good, as if that explained why I was with him at all, as we broke up and got back together for months.

It was spring by the time I could last a few weeks sober. John Carlo had gone out on one of those Friday nights when we didn't know if we were together anymore or not. I went to every AA meeting I could find, lingering around The Lambda Center in fear that I'd go out and find him and do a bump with him or not find him and know he'd hooked up with some Decatur Street whore. I went to an Al-Anon meeting and cried about our relationship not being the way it was anymore and that I couldn't find the acceptance for the way I'd become a Tuesday Girl, waiting for him to call until I'd want to slit my wrists, even though the time I'd tried it hadn't even worked. You were supposed to find acceptance, they were always saying at meetings, but on Fridays all I could think about were the nights when we blew lines until dawn, fucking and crashing together while the first birds whistled 'loser.'

When the meeting let out, I went looking for L.T. who had a bunch of these yellow Percocet pills. He was sitting in Mimi's with a Budweiser. I had forgotten the smell of dead beer on wood. The barflies glistened above their drinks. Oh, how I loved seeing them. I asked L.T. for the pills, but he had eaten them all.

"That sucks. Why did you eat them all?"

"The pain, baby. The pain," he said, as if that wasn't obvious. His pain was there, crackling around his edges; I just didn't know the source.

I was telling myself I should leave and call my sponsor when I saw John Carlo. His eyes were dark pools; the lines on his face were etched so deeply that night that nobody would believe he was 37. There weren't any single women around.

"Will you walk me home, cupcake?" he asked.

I liked when he called me that.

He'd moved into this water-stained apartment an old woman had been living in, and she'd left him her furniture, old couches and chairs with throw pillows embroidered with slogans about grandmothers. It seemed more like he was house-sitting, and I realized he hadn't had his own apartment since I'd known him, but had shuffled from room to room in Aaron's guesthouse and then to my place when Aaron kicked him out.

He chopped up some lines and handed me the straw. There was nothing to say.

The coke had no effect on me. I couldn't decide if I was relieved or frustrated.

He needed to touch me then. I'd seen him wired like that before, and I loved him for needing me, but he was as far away as if he'd broken up with me again, and his shitty coke wasn't helping me reach him.

Once, when he still lived with Aaron, he'd ended it, saying it was because my sobriety made him feel guilty. I'd relapsed over it, and after a 40 bag and a fifth of Jim Beam, I'd broken down Aaron's front door. I fought all five of the cops who came when he called them before they took me to the psych ward. He had said he'd go with me right before I peed myself, but he didn't get in the ambulance and wouldn't answer the phone when I called.

But on this night, he'd forgotten about that. Some music was playing, a song about drugs and pain, the kind of song that gives you hope for the singer, that makes you feel like he's been miraculously cured, but the song wasn't ending for John Carlo. He was living in it, turning on the television to watch soft porn with the sound off.

A man in a cowboy hat tittie-fucked a woman against some flowery wallpaper in a fleabag motel room. I couldn't believe the cowboy hat stayed on his head. The movie was called *The Lost Cowboy*, somehow implying that the man had wandered away from the ranch and into this prostitute's arms.

John Carlo was groping me, and I put my arms around him, trying to send to him whatever love I had for him, but he was radioactive and couldn't absorb what I had to give.

"What's your sex drive like tonight?" he asked.

"You could have said 'I love you,'" I replied.

"I love you."

But I couldn't do it that night. I'd go back to him over and over again until I'd get sick of him, but then his truck would get stolen, or he'd cook some cocaine and smoke it and scare himself, and he'd find me again, and we'd take care of each other for a while, but that night my heart broke for him and for Jules and for Jack as I let myself out. I stood outside Smitty's, the dirtiest bar on the block, for a long time before shuffling home.

***

Recovery was like that. I never knew how I was feeling from one moment to the next, whether I'd be crying for a drink or saying Foxhole prayers of gratitude. I'd be fighting about plasma or running to The Lambda Center where someone would tell me that junkie pride and junkie shame were one in the same. I wanted to be a little planet, hard and close to the sun in my little orbit. I wasn't afraid that if I'd go back out I would die. It's that I would live.

WINDOWS
by Dana Harrison-Tidwell

I need these windows. Before, only six French doors
wrapped in privacy shutters (five perma-locked, one dead-bolted
twice) kept them all out, kept us all in. Voices leaked through gaps
to a constant muffled background laughter as hurricane parties
went forward as planned. I uprooted last-minute from the narrow
slave quarter. I was afraid looking through that French door full of
glass I might shatter into 12 parts of myself & float out, lost among
shredded banana leaves and naked bougainvillea. I was scared to
cross the threshold from door to shutter. The last phone call for
weeks shook me as I hesitated near a latch, glided a finger along
the key's teeth. I, startled, cut my hand on a broken bottom pane,
sank barely breathing to the floor, stigmata'd palm flat and fingers
fanned out and oozing more blood into the carpet, wondering how
many martyrs would be found hiding the wounds of thousands
they left behind or could not save. No wandering from the others
- they're all there in the eyes - and can't we all just try to forget? I
need these windows to study the purple star-shaped scar licking my
love line, my heart line, my lifeline, all futures interrupted. If I can
just find the trick, I'll slide right through— half mirrored portrait,
half framed landscape— right through glass and catch fruit from the
chinaberry tree I used to park beneath, berries that fell away waxy,
like the skin over dead eyes, shrinking inward, discarding warmth.
I could string them into a rosary, thumb ticking off the 250 rainless
days in this hitch along I-10 where the car ran out of gas and I ran

out of money and it seemed as good a place as any to finish bleeding out, which I didn't because I wasn't brave enough to reopen my hand down through the wrist. I could tick off the occasional distant lightning and still have time to make sense of latches and locks. Maybe what's coming now will blow right through me, scouring clean bones and hidden fistfuls of Xanax. I flinch at thunderclaps and rush to fill the tub with water, the sinks, the 20-gallon carboys. I keep a suspicious eye on the arroyo next to my house. It's that it's 3:00 a.m., and I am unnervingly vacant in the silent moments, no unhinged laughter seeping through cracks, and sleep is somehow harder to find in quiet, and I'm distracted by stars I never saw before for the glare of the city, and I am wondering where all the voices landed. It's that I press my forehead against gritty glass, feeling static pulling me into it, and I squint the hares outside into the shapes of partygoers. Then I hear the ruthless scream of a telephone somewhere. I look away. I lose myself.

HOLES
Andrea Boll

There are plenty of items hard to come by since the hurricane: a gas station with a working air pump for my tires with slow leaks from the nails of gutted houses, two empty washers on a Sunday morning, a hamburger after 10 p.m. An abortion, however, is not. The first clinic in the phone book exists. It makes sense. This is not a time to be bringing children into the world.

The nurse asks me what type I want: the pill or surgical. Both are five hundred dollars. Medicaid, she explains, will not cover it. Cash only.

I laugh. Of course. Everything in this city is cash only right now.

I choose the pill. I know the surgical kind will leave me doubled over for the day, and there is nobody to pick me up. She gives me a 10 a.m. appointment.

The clinic is on St. Charles Avenue in what appears to be a church. I sit in my station wagon for a long time, convinced it will be a trick—as soon as I walk in, a righteous mob of pro-lifers will ambush me, take me to some Christian retreat in Arkansas to have the baby. I curse the diaphragm that failed me. I curse Mateo whom I can't get a hold of. I curse New Orleans for being so fucked up, because if everything and everyone weren't wobbling on the edge of chaos, I might have it.

But it isn't a trick. Women are coming in and out of the front door. The windows are a menacing, bulletproof black.

Inside it is too cold. All of us are dressed for the heat of June, not sixty degrees. For three hours, I wait among the scowling and shivering women, nothing to read except pamphlets on STD's, Preventing HIV, and Prenatal Care. One woman, a girl really, slaps her little boy every time he drops his pacifier.

I think about Mateo and the Night-Blooming Cereus—how I should have gone to check on them last night. When my daughter, Vienna, and I went a week ago, they were just starting to bud. Mateo had said they would bloom anywhere from three to seven days after the bud first appeared. He was the one who found the entire yard of them in lower Ninth Ward and made me promise I would take care of them. He said that no matter what, I had to watch them bloom because it was one of the botanical marvels of the world. "It's proof," he had said, "that God is much more concerned with flowers than humans."

Finally, the nurse calls my name. She takes my heart rate and weight. I sign a paper saying I have been counseled on the risks and am aware of what I am doing. She then takes me to the doctor, an old white man, who looks at me with a mix of disdain and boredom before telling me to get on the examination table for an ultrasound.

He points to the fetus that looks likes like a very tiny hole on the left side of my uterus, a black star alone in universe. Of course. Everything in New Orleans is a hole, holes in the shapes of things and people who used to be here. Like the oak trees. One day they were large and spread above my broken house. The next day, the Army Corps of Engineers came, chopped them up, and carted them away limb by limb to the anonymous necropolis of this disaster. I didn't even realize they were dead. A lot of things are like that, though, just shells of their former selves you can't tell are dead until somebody tells you. Now when I look up, all I see are tree-shaped holes in the sky. They make me think I might never live in my house again.

"I'd say you're about five weeks pregnant," the doctor tells me.

He is right. It was almost exactly five weeks ago when Mateo left to Nicaragua, to finish his research on orchids, the same night he brought me to the yard of the Night-Blooming Cereus. Vienna had gone with her daddy for the weekend. Alone in the hotel room, Mateo and I fucked wildly above the city, tricking a spirit from the land of the unborn that there was enough love to bring him or her into the world of the living.

The doctor leaves, and a half an hour later, the nurse comes in. "Okay," she says, "we'll see you tomorrow."

"What do you mean?" I ask.

"The nurse at the front desk didn't tell you? In Louisiana, state law requires a woman to wait 24 hours after her first visit before she can have the procedure."

I close my eyes to keep from breaking down. I am going to have to ask Thaddeus, my ex-husband and Vienna's daddy, to watch her again. The three hours of babysitting will cost me a week's worth of sanity. Abortions are also easier to find than childcare.

I open my eyes and notice how tired the nurse looks. "Don't worry," she says. "You won't have to wait like this tomorrow. We'll have the pills waiting for you."

I drive back to the Hilton where I have been living since November. The Environmental Protection Agency paid for it when I began working for them after I was laid off from teaching Botany at UNO. Mostly I was hired to take soil and water samples from around the city, but I spend a lot of my time doing field research on the changes in flora and fauna since the hurricane. I take Vienna to different parts of the city where we wander in our rain boots through the yards of the flooded houses, taking notes of any new species and documenting the growth of old ones. Lately, I've been monitoring the egrets that have come to live in the marshy front yards of Gentilly and the profusion of fennel bushes. I discovered two species of ferns typically found in Chiapas living all over Lakeview and monkey tail vine, common to Costa Rica, growing over a house in Carrollton.

At the hotel, Vienna and her daddy are asleep in front of Sesame Street. He does not know about my pregnancy.

"Your boyfriend called," Thaddeus says with his eyes closed. "I told him we are back together and not to call here anymore." He laughs and gets up.

"Thanks for watching Vienna," I say to him. "I appreciate it."

Thaddeus comes over and sniffs me. "You went to see him, didn't you? You call me to babysit so you can go fuck him. I can smell him on you."

"No Thaddeus, I did not go see him," I say and prepare for the argument that is always the same. The demise of our marriage is my fault. He had to party through the four years of our marriage because I was in love with someone else the entire time: Mateo.

This is not completely true. Yes, once before the storm, way before Thaddeus, when I was finishing up grad school, I loved Mateo, also a botany student at LSU. But he was married then with a son that he was not willing to leave. So I closed up that heart and put it away. In Thaddeus, I found a new one. He was nothing like the dark, serious Mateo. Thaddeus distrusted anything too rational, believed science was a myth, and wanted only to have a good time and play the violin. We got married, got pregnant, and had Vienna. Right before the storm, we bought a house in Gentilly. Mateo, I heard, got divorced. I kept waiting for Thaddeus to party less like he had promised, but the opposite happened. Because he had to go all the way downtown to play gigs and hang out, he left the house early and came back late or not at all.

At first I thought the storm and its aftermath was going to save our marriage. Driving contraflow down the I-10 West, I felt, for the first time since loving Mateo, that life was interesting. The first adventure in our family lore we would tell our grandchildren.

We made it all the way to Colorado where his uncle was waiting for us. After a month, however, the mountains, Thaddeus said, made him crazy. He went back to New Orleans with the promise that he would find a job and a place to live so Vienna and I could return, too. But when he arrived here, he found his former addictions instead: whisky, cocaine, and barrooms. By living in our station wagon and playing his violin on the street, his unemployment check and FEMA money were enough to sustain him.

It took me a month to realize the only way I was getting back to New Orleans was if I found my own way. So I got the job with the EPA and we moved into our suite on the 35th floor.

Thaddeus did not join us. He said the hotel room made him claustrophobic and preferred the car. The cocaine gave him a hard, entitled edge. He needed to be able to play his music on the street at any time because playing the violin at any time was how he dealt with the state of New Orleans. He acted like he was the only one with a New Orleans-shaped hole in his heart.

But I loved him still, or at least, was willing to try to love him. And it was then that I first starting thinking of Mateo again, understanding how a child can chain you to another person with iron links that have nothing to do with love. At first, I gave Thaddeus his space, hoping he'd come around. I let him take baths in the hotel. I gave him my food stamps. And when he would leave, I made Vienna Mac-n-Cheese on the hot plate I had smuggled into our room and tell her stories about princesses who save themselves. It wasn't until he took the food stamps and traded them for cocaine that I stopped trying.

Like our relationship, our house did not make it through the flood intact. Thaddeus had promised to have the house gutted when he left Colorado. Said he'd do it himself. When January came and it was still festering in its own filth and mold, Thaddeus wanted us to get back together. He was going to be a changed man and wanted to take me on a "first date" to gut the house, the first step in rebuilding our lives together. He had even asked his aunt over in Slidell to watch Vienna.

I waited at the broken house for five hours, amazed and pained at what water could do to the solidness of life: change completely its constitution. Wood bends and buckles, fabric becomes wall, walls crumble like dirt into your hands, love rots into an indecipherable pulp. And since I thought we'd ride back to the

166

Hilton together, I had no ride home. The bus had stopped running at five, so I walked from Gentilly, tracing the water line lower and lower, to where it finally disappeared in the Sixth Ward. I turned down North Rampart, and there was Mateo, outside Hula Mae's, waiting to do laundry.

When I saw him, I just sat down on the sidewalk and cried. I told him everything that had happened since Katrina.

Mateo called his friend who said he'd gut my house for three hundred dollars. He would do it the next day. "It's that easy," Mateo said.

When Thaddeus came to the hotel later that night, drunk and high, he didn't even remember we had planned a date. I had to call hotel security to make him leave.

Thaddeus looks at me. "You're lying about something. I can feel it in my heart."

"Please Thaddeus. I have to email my boss before Vienna wakes up."

"Lucinda," he says, making his voice sweet, "I know you still love me. Let me come and be with y'all. Vienna needs her daddy and so do you. Look at you. You look like shit."

I shake my head. "Before I would even consider taking you back, you would have to sober up and get a job." I know he would never be sober.

With one hand, Thaddeus grabs my neck and pushes me against the wall. The thumping sound wakes Vienna, who begins to cry. "Fuck you, you fucking bitch. When you stop being a fucking whore, I'll stop drinking." He leans closer and grips my neck tighter. "Where's Mateo, huh?" he whispers. "Is he fucking his wife? Just wait, he's going to break your heart again, and when he does, don't come looking for me."

I punch him in his stomach. He gasps and lets go of my neck. I used to cower when he came home violent in a whiskey cocaine rage, but now I fight back. I push him with my leg, and he falls, hitting the edge of the desk.

"You bitch," he screams, holding his side. "I think you cracked my rib."

"Get out." I pick up Vienna who is still crying.

"Whore. You're lucky I don't knock you out," he says before leaving.

I decide just to take Vienna with me to the clinic. Miraculously, the pills are ready. After, I drive Vienna to the park and swallow the first set that will block my body from making any more progesterone. I wait the required hour and take the second set that will make my uterus contract to expel the fetus. I'm expecting horrific pain, but it's nothing— similar to the cramping before my period. When the blood comes, it isn't that excessive. It almost feels natural, as if my body has been waiting to do this all along, but didn't know how.

That evening, Thaddeus shows up at the hotel room with a pizza. "I got a job," he says. "I deliver pizzas now for Angeli's. I'm halfway to the man you want me to be."

When he leaves, Vienna starts crying for him to come back, Mateo does not call, and I can no longer breathe the recycled air of the hotel.

"Come on, Vienna," I say. "Let's go see if Mateo's flowers have bloomed."

168

We cross the canal to the lower Nine and turn down Forstall. I drive all the way to the end without recognizing anything. I turn back around and look for the brick house, the only one on the street that had not shifted after the barge broke the levee. It takes me a minute to recognize the brick house shaped hole gaping in the darkness. For some reason, only the stairs to the porch are still there. We get out of the car.

"Yeah!" Vienna yells. "Mateo's flowers." She climbs the steps and then jumps into the dirt where a porch used to be. She runs to the backyard.

"Mama, the flowers are here!" she yells. "Hurry."

I run to meet her, already writing Mateo a letter in my head about their appearance.

She holds out her hand where there is a wilted, white mess of a flower. I look around. They are all like that, dead and barely hanging on.

ESTHER
Lucas Diaz-Medina

Maldito sea, she cursed mentally. She'd been doing this for weeks now without fully realizing that she was doing it—cursing her husband, her life, this city. If only she were home, a place where she could turn to friends, to family. Two years in New Orleans, with a major hurricane slashing into those years like a scythe into a cotton sheet hanging on a clothesline, had not been enough time to make friends. Not that Esther would have made the effort in that time, even if there were no hurricane. She was naturally reserved and quiet. She rarely spoke up to her husband, even to defend herself in an argument.

But these two years in New Orleans had been terrible. At least in New York City she could walk into Spanish-speaking shops, could leave her children with second cousins from the old neighborhoods back home when she needed to run a fast errand. In New York City, she could walk or take a taxi right outside her apartment door to get where she needed to go.

No en esta maldita ciudad, she thought to herself. Getting around was impossible without a car, and she didn't know how to drive. She couldn't go anywhere without her husband taking her, though she had often considered taking the long walk to the local grocery store. From the car drive alone it appeared to be far away. Once, when her husband was gone on business for five days, she considered taking the walk. She believed she knew, from the many direct trips in the car, exactly where the store was located, but she never stepped out of the front door. It wasn't so much any personal fear she had for herself that kept her from trying the trip. She believed herself to be capable. Doña Castilla had said so once when Esther was a teenager, and if Doña Castilla believed in her, then that was enough for Esther. Everyone back home knew that Doña Castilla's observations, when made, carried the most solemn weight. Still, that truth, so far away, felt feather thin in New Orleans.

No, it was something else that kept her from trying the trip. A self-imposed concern she had for her children. A need to keep them safe. And in her exiled thoughts she believed that taking a risk on a long walk in a direction she was barely certain about was not a good risk to take with her children. She chose to stay home, always. This is how she had lived the last two years. From first arrival, through the evacuation weeks (which even now seem like a blur that barely happened), to the return to this place, she felt alone and trapped. Her children, for whom she lived, gave her strength. This is what she told herself while she explored in her heart the reasons for keeping her marriage. José, in most ways, was a good husband, she thought. He cared for her in ways even her own mother had not. But lately, it had become different, soured. Ever since they came to New Orleans. No, she remembered accurately. It started the months prior to leaving New York City. It started when she began her crying spells after he informed her that they were going to Louisiana, to a city she'd never heard of called Nueva Orleans.

¿Por qué diablo vinimos aquí? The job he took wasn't an improvement over what he had in New York City. What drew him here?

It didn't take Esther long to figure that out, at least, in her own estimation. She wasn't born yesterday, she told herself the

172

day she realized what was going on. However, she did doubt herself—for months, then Katrina hit and her silly thoughts were thrown away with everything else she thought that was banal and ill-conceived. They drove to friends and family in New York City. Stayed there four weeks before driving back. Esther pleaded with her husband to forget New Orleans, but he forced his family back down to this place. What could she do?

Their small home had some damage, but nothing they couldn't live with. Life took on a surreal aspect to it when they returned, living as they did among debris, limited supplies, boarded up houses, missing neighbors, and fear of the next hurricane season. It didn't flood where they lived, and with the exception of wind damage, most of the homes in the neighborhood she lived in were filled with people six months after the storm. She noticed this around the same time she noticed José acting strange again. Whatever short respite the storm had offered her family, it came to an end. This time, when it came back, rather than begin to accept her place as a wife and a woman with little recourse or alternative, she began to think that she should consider leaving him.

At first, these thoughts were filled with exciting fantasies in which she angrily expressed an ultimatum to José, and which he always accepted, pledging eternal faith and commitment to her. The scenery changed each time she dreamt it, but the result was always the same. She would savor these little fantasies while she went about her household business. Often, during dinner, she would quietly envision her husband, who would be sitting across the table from her, apologizing for not being what she had hoped him to be in their marriage. But these visions didn't satisfy her growing displeasure with him, which had in all honesty been growing for many years now, though Esther hated to admit this to herself. Her mother knew before she agreed to the marriage, and had even said so on her wedding night.

"Esther," her mother said quietly. She was busy pinning up a portion of Esther's hair that refused to stay in position that night. "*¿Sabes que José es como tu papá?*" Esther tried asking her what she meant, but that was all she would say. The way her mother said it was intended to be understood as an unfortunate and potentially unsettling similarity. José was like Esther's father. This could have meant many things, but Esther believed she knew what her mother intended to say and chose to ignore it. José loved her, and that was enough. She loved José. But now it didn't seem so easy to believe this. Yes, she still loved him, even enjoyed him when they took their clothes off beneath the sheets, but even this was changing. Changing in an unexpected way. Making her feel, in the last few months, as if she were an unwanted house cat that required the occasionally petting. Yes, it was changing, and she knew it. She knew it even before it began to manifest itself in the extra hours at work, the mysterious new smells on his clothes, the suddenly protective manner in which he emptied his pockets as he undressed.

At first she thought it was the storm, that they were both suffering mental stress—exhaustion from living in a world that bore little resemblance to the normal life they led before the storm. She tried to not pay any attention to it, knowing that when the water rises, it's best to learn to float than try to keep it off the sand. But it began, ever so slightly, to gnaw at her, eating at the thin film she'd created over the years, the film under which she had lived out her fiction, until eventually, it hurt.

This happened suddenly, taking her by surprise. When her husband announced he had to go on a last minute two-week trip to Santo Domingo on some supposed business deal, she clutched her rib as if she'd been kicked. It was an involuntary reaction, which for a moment created a humble scene—Esther stumbling backwards against the bedroom wall, gasping for air while her husband reached forward, his heavy body almost graceful as it leaned in her direction with sincere concern and alarm. But this lasted less than three seconds. Disgust, which didn't go unnoticed by Esther, flashed across José's face, ever so slightly, when he realized she was just reacting in a feminine way to his news.

"*Coño, mujer. No te pongas así. ¿Por qué diablo lloras?*" He was beside himself with quick anger when Esther burst into sudden tears. He looked at her, paced the room back and forth in front of her, left the bedroom to check on their children, returned and stared at her a while longer, until at last he spoke, this time calmly, without anger. "*Mira. Es una gran oportunidad. Tengo que ir.*"

Esther, however, was not buying it. She didn't believe him when he explained that it was a business trip. Didn't believe for a minute that it was as important as he tried to make it sound. From the moment it came out of his mouth, she knew it was a lie—two weeks, and without his family. Two weeks—as if it were something he did all the time. Two weeks—as if it were as simple as driving down the block. Why couldn't they all go? Why couldn't he take his family? Two weeks—which he said as casually as saying her name. Last time he had an extended trip planned, the entire family went. As soon as it came out of his mouth, Esther knew something was different, wasn't right. She knew everything those two words signified. Knew that for him to utter them as casually as he did that it was the end of whatever it was they had been trying to build for the last ten years.

That night, as he made his arrangements on the phone for the first flight out the next morning, Esther slept with her children— falling asleep beside Junior on the bottom bunk. She dreamt in fits, having bouts of nightmares and euphoric fantasies. Her children, who slept deeply in the same room with her, were spared their mother's dream battles as she raged with herself long into the night. In one dream, she lay exactly in the same place and in the same way her real body laid, on her side beside her son. She opened her eyes and there was José, smiling at her with his arm outstretched, imploring her to take his hand. Rather than lift her arm and place her fingers in his, she closed her eyes and dug her nose deep into her son's neck. When she looked up again, José was gone.

Esther didn't know how it happened. She had not set an alarm clock. From within a deep dream in which she was back home, a carefree teenager from the back country fields of La Romana who was being courted by a big city Dominican, she heard noises. Sounded like someone moving around, someone doing things in the house. And it came to her that José was packing. It was not quite dawn yet, with still no sign of light from the arriving morning.

For a moment she considered letting it all pass, the way she'd learned to do so over the years in a marriage that grew increasingly difficult to accept. When the small infractions began, when the little oddities took shape inside her mind, giving her cues to the growing scents of displeasure and contempt that began to characterize José's behavior toward her, she often became even

176

more subservient, more quiet, and hoped that she was dreaming it all, that she was imagining it all and it would pass. But it never passed. It quieted down sometimes, but it came back. Came back in little instances so difficult to capture that she often wondered if she was going crazy. This time, however, something inside awoke. Maybe it was the storm. The ordeal of having lived through the nightmare, the suspense, the trying return, the disappointing return, all of this had taught her something that she'd been unable to act on all her life—that she was made of something grittier than she'd ever admitted to herself or ever shown. It was inside, and she was prepared to let it out, to show it. She could not allow this moment to come into and out of her life quietly.

When she heard him enter the bathroom, she moved into the hallway and inspected what he'd done so far. His luggage was in the living room, some of his clothes thrown onto the back of the dining chair. Esther felt an urge to take his clothes and throw them into the garbage can. She wanted to go into the kitchen, grab a knife and slash into the luggage bag. But she resisted. Fixing her eyes on the picture of the Virgin Mary they had conspicuously placed behind the entertainment center, she waited. She stared at Christ's mother while her insides ignited into a frenzy of molten activity. All her life she'd lived a devout, Catholic wife's life, following what she believed was the correct way to take on her marriage. Living in New York City, and maybe even more so in New Orleans, she'd begun to see how differently life could be lived. She saw how men certainly were not interested in upholding any old religious traditions. Questions began to enter her mind; questions she'd never dared ask back home when she was still under her mother's roof. At the same time that she felt the excitement of this newfound strength, this potential independence was weaving its way through her body. She fully understood how frightening this new life could be. She didn't know the language, didn't drive and didn't have any money. Supported completely by her husband, she was incapable of living on her own in the States. What would she do if they separated? Return to La Romana? Go back to her mother? Go to New York City, where her aunts could take her in?

Esther lost herself in these thoughts and when José emerged from the bathroom, she went to him not as an angry woman demanding his attention—which in their marriage was still something Esther had not brought herself to demonstrate, but as the woman she had always been.

"*José, por favor,*" she said. "I won't be able to," she half whispered in Spanish. He knew this. He knew that she couldn't go it alone in this town without him.

"Esther, don't be ridiculous," José answered. He grabbed her hands, which had thrown themselves onto his muscular left arm. "Now, let me finish packing, or I'll miss my plane."

"But why can't we go? Why can't you bring your family, like last time?"

"You know," José answered, "that we have to watch our money. We can't just buy four tickets like that as if money flowed through the faucet. Besides, if all goes well from this trip, we'll be able to go back and forth anytime we want." In the past this comment may have been enough to calm Esther down, but not this time. This time she merely slapped the noise of it down before it even reached her ears.

"In the meantime," she said, "how do you expect me to live here? How will I make it without you?"

José didn't answer. He moved to the living room and began to hurriedly pack up. Esther stopped just paces away from him; her arms crossed now, the bubbling insides beginning to press her. José noticed this. He stopped, only briefly, and looked at her.

"Esther, please," he pleaded—a hint of concern in his voice. "Don't get like that. I'll be back quick. You'll see."

Esther surprised herself. She snorted a half-repressed giggle. It was the sort of giggle a worldly person makes when confronted with a scam, no matter where it takes place. The wizened woman's contempt for simple lies. "And what will I do for two entire weeks?" she asked, but not in the same pleading way she had only recently spoken. This time, she wasn't asking him in order to get an answer. She was simply asking it aloud, repeating into the universe what she'd been thinking and worrying about only minutes before when she waited to confront him.

José returned to his luggage. He hurriedly packed the few remaining items that were left. "Don't be ridiculous. The same as always—take care of Junior and Carmen."

Again, the same surprised, contemptuous small laugh. "How lovely," she said, "while the father goes whoring in Santo Domingo." It came out suddenly, despite herself. It was the first time she'd ever openly accused him of being unfaithful. "I won't forgive you," she added, knowing as she said it that she meant this—meant it no matter what happened if he walked out of that door this morning.

José didn't seem to pick up her intent. He simply went on, impatiently, now obviously frustrated with her. "Look, for the last time. It's only business. Only business." He turned around and closed his luggage after putting in the last item of clothing. While he did this, Esther studied his large back and wondered why the hell it was that she ever married him. For a minute, while she watched him, she felt both the sadness of the situation and the anger bubbling from her new self, the new self trying desperately to emerge. José, however, seemed to suddenly not be in as much of a hurry. Esther waited, curious about what he was trying to do, trying to think about. She knew that this sudden quiet moment meant that he was trying to say something, thinking of a way to break into a difficult suggestion or idea, or comment.

He turned around and held out a yellow scrap of paper. "Here, take this," he said.

Esther didn't move, her arms still crossed. "What's this?"

"It's Eva's number."

Esther had heard the name before. José had mentioned her in the same conversations about work meetings and work dinners. He'd mentioned her in the context of party invitations and other social affairs. Even threw her name out once when in anger he asked Esther why she couldn't be more like Eva. Esther had not thought much about these individual incidents, had accepted them as she accepted everything else in her life—with stoic silence. But not this time. At the mention of her name something that was bubbling inside Esther erupted and rose to her head. Her reaction was swift and it surprised her husband.

"What for?" she asked.

"In case ..." José began, but was unable to finish because Esther quickly cut him off. His voice sounded meek, too soft to be the voice of the large man who had protected her, cared for her most of her life.

"In case what?" she demanded.

"You know. In case you need..." but again, Esther cut him off.

"You bastard," she laughed. She watched him as he dropped the yellow sheet of paper that he was trying to put in her hands. He picked it up and again feebly tried to give it to her, but Esther had had enough of this. She was not going to accept her husband placing her care in the hands of one of his women.

José tried again, still pleading his case. "I've told you, Esther. Eva is a friend. You're going to need her. Please take this and call her. I have to go." He took one of Esther's hands and put the paper in it, cupping it closed with his own large paws.

Esther took the paper and threw it on the floor. What was she, she asked herself, a child? She could get along fine without some whore of his coming by to help the little helpless, subdued wife.

José reacted with quick anger. He picked up the paper and again placed it in her hand, this time grabbing her closer toward him. "Damn it, Esther, please," he said, not pleading this time but urging nonetheless, his fear for her evident on his face while he angrily spat out that she shouldn't be stubborn, that she didn't speak English, that she didn't know her way around, for crying out loud, she hadn't even learned how to go to the grocery store nearby. He knew that she would need help. Esther could see this in his face sitting just beneath the reddened, taut cheeks and clenched teeth.

For a moment she considered speaking aloud the ultimatum she had already decided in her heart.

Sales por esa puerta hoy, José, y nunca te lo perdono, she thought. If only he could see what she was thinking and keep himself from walking out of that door because if he left, now, as he was certainly intent on doing, she would end the marriage. She knew it as sure as she knew that today was the beginning of a new life, as sure as she knew that Esther Carmen Marmol de Vidriano, only daughter of Consuelo Marmol from La Romana in the Dominican Republic, would get out of this hell hole of a town called New Orleans where a Latino had as hard a time as a fish on land. She would move on and learn how to make it. And she would do this alone, if she had to.

As her husband gave her a perfunctory kiss on the cheeks and turned his back toward her, she made an amusing observation. She may not like it here, but New Orleans had taught her how to face this man's back who at some point in her life had been her husband.

Boo
Anne Gisleson

The kids are already shedding pieces of their costumes. A gypsy scarf weaves through a stand of ragged cast iron plants, a plastic sword pierces the storm drain already clogged with oak leaves. It's a too-hot Halloween and parents shift around with their babies or glance distractedly about the loose groups of wrangling, masquerading children. Families are meeting at the park on Elysian Fields because somebody has put a map together of households in the neighborhood that agreed in advance to give out treats. This arrangement sort of depresses the Mother, as she remembers her childhood Halloweens for their spontaneous thrills, their safe and theatrical creepiness. The half-sheet map she clutches to the stroller was poorly photocopied and hard to read, the grid of her own neighborhood somehow disorienting.

She understands the parents' impulse, though. Marigny and Bywater still hug the fringes. A few blocks away, on the other side of St. Claude Avenue, the Reconstruction is faltering, large swaths still in ruins. After a few quiet, idealistic months after the storm, crime came back and back and back. And night after night, in the sweet heavy quiet after bedtime, over glasses of wine, across kitchen tables, under cracked plaster bedroom ceilings, parents who stayed exhaust themselves on whirring treadmills of rationalizations. They are gamely making a go at normalcy, gamely moving forward, all for the sake of their children. They are also losing it, self-medicating and stealthily pondering leaving town.

"Who are you supposed to be?" one of the fathers asks the Mother as she adjusts the stroller so the Baby, freshly napped, can sit up. "Courtney Love?"

She'd palmed white pancake makeup over her face while rushing to get out of the house to pick up S. from kindergarten, smeared hasty black circles around her eyes and ratted out her hair with a plastic fork as she packed the diaper bag.

"God no. I'm supposed to be *ghoulish*. What are you?"

"I don't know. Just. Whatever. Spooky?" He shrugs his shoulders, helpless to explain himself. He's wearing a hard hat with a bunch of different things duct-taped to it, a few small stuffed animals, a key chain, a crushed beer can, possibly a real animal bone. It's spooky in a disturbing, deranged kind of way.

"You just kind of look crazy."

He's an architect who lives nearby in a half-million dollar Creole townhouse with a set of hyperactive blond twin boys and a wife she's never met.

"That's all right. I feel crazy," He says with a sad, all too familiar half-smile.

The kids' costumes are very straightforward and unmistakable, princesses, pirates, a couple of Spidermen, witches. At least the ghoulish/Courtney Love thing works with the Baby's costume. Since it was too hot for the tiny monkey suit his aunt had bought, she put a black Ramones onesie on him and kissed him all over his face with hot red lipstick so he looked like a tiny bald rock star. Just after she'd done it, she realized, mortified, that she had used "color-stay" lipstick and that later she'll most likely be scrubbing and scrubbing his perfect, delicate skin with a washcloth to get it to come off.

186

She watches her stepson, S., hassle the monkey bars on the dark green play equipment, which is rusted, scarred and swaddled in duct tape, probably by the architect, to minimize any potential injury. The equipment area is edged by stumps of crepe myrtle trees and thinned out oaks. With much of the tree canopy gone throughout the city, the quality of light has changed, buildings and stretches of sky re-exposed after decades, even centuries, of verdant concealment, glare intruding where there once was much needed shade. A fence topped with thousands of dull cast iron daggers encloses the park. Across Royal Street, a nursing home broods over its south end, a haphazard mid-century monolith studded with window units, ambulances often idling expectantly in front of its long striped awning.

S. runs up to the Mother in his Garfield costume, an orange sweat suit that his father had painted stripes onto the night before, to compensate for having to work late Halloween.

"Mom! I forgot the bag. I forgot the bag in aftercare." S.'s face begins its quick crumple into full-on wet-cheeked despair.

"What bag? What are you talking about, honey?"

He explains breathlessly that they had all been given special trick-or-treat bags by the ladies in aftercare. "We can get another one. You don't need that bag. It doesn't matter, sweetheart."

She reaches underneath his orange hood to rub his hair, recognizing her lie. Of course it matters. She just doesn't want to go all the way back to the school. More kids are gathering around the play equipment. More maps are being handed out to parents. Things are about to get going. But his mind had locked itself on The Special Bag and his eyes no longer focus on anything around him.

She knows that with these long-anticipated holidays, the possibility of disappointment is ratcheted-up. Tomorrow, it will be over except the candy hangover and when he comes across the bag on one of the grey folding chairs in the St. Paul's Lutheran basement, he will become overcome with regret and sadness. Besides, in trying to get the baby out of the house she'd forgotten to grab a treat bag for him at all.

"All right, let's go, but aftercare closes in like…" She checks the time on her cell phone in the stroller's cup holder. "Fifteen minutes."

As he runs for his green Razor scooter, she makes hurried goodbyes and pledges to meet up with the group on the route but as she reaches the edge of the park away from the colorful fracas, she is relieved to not have to walk with the crowd, negotiating the sidewalks with a glut of strollers and shrieking kids. She's still relatively new to motherhood, not entirely comfortable with its topography, which is far more chaotic and unforgiving than she'd expected. The Baby is quiet and sparkling, checking out the passing oak branches in his obscene face paint.

Aftercare, in the aboveground basement below the 19th century Lutheran church, is where the kids go whose parents work past 3:15. It's run by Ninth Ward ladies who grew up and raised kids in the neighborhood and then watched them leave for suburbs, like most of their friends and neighbors had done over the decades. They'd witnessed the crime and the shifting demographics, the blacks, and now the gays and a smattering of younger white families and professionals and bohemian types. When she first started picking up S. right after the storm, the Mother was a recently married, insecure stepmom and pregnant with her first baby. But when the ladies greeted her with "Good afternoon, Mamma" when she came to get S., they made her feel as though she did somehow belong to that club after all, no questions asked. Though raised Catholic uptown, she will always be grateful to the downtown Lutherans, how their pastor stayed to administer throughout everything, how they got their school back up and running seven weeks after the storm, how when she showed up to register S. there was no electricity but there was the antiseptic smell of cleaning fluid, teachers on step stools in shorts wiping down shelves, on their hands and knees scrubbing the terrazzo floors.

S. scoots ahead though the empty, darkening parking lot and returns with The Bag. It's the size of an envelope and made of cheap cellophane printed with black and orange bats. But she sees why he wanted it, why it's an essential part of the formula.

The sun abandons the city to its Halloween dealings. The Mother and S. and the Baby stroll long unlit blocks of Burgundy Street back towards Elysian Fields, dogs rushing the chain-link fences between darkened houses, barking through the old cast iron vent covers under porches and sending S. and his scooter careening towards parked cars.

"Hey look mom, over there!" Down Spain Street, a light bobs in a doorway and they move toward it.

In the recessed entrance of a fastidiously restored Victorian side hall, chandelier-lit, windows hung with deep red silk shantung, a man swings a Coleman camping lantern like Paul Revere.

"You're only our second visitors of the evening. We've been trying to send you signals." His French cuffs glow in the lantern light. Behind him another man lifts a tray from a marble-topped sideboard and extends a crisply wrapped black cat cookie toward S.

189

"Wait! What do you say?"

"Trick or Treat!" S. jumps up and down, tail thumping the brick steps.

A spasm of relief and gratitude in the Mother. It's official now. S. got to say it.

"And one for him." The man holding the tray approaches the stroller with a pumpkin cookie. He, too, sports French-cuffs.

"He's not eating solids yet," the Mother says, "but thanks."

The men look at each, one shrugging and the other shaking his head.

They turn down Franklin, a dim block not usually taken, and suddenly they are knee-deep in weeds that have all but vanquished the sidewalk. She knows they should turn back but they push on, S. walking his scooter and complaining about getting burrs, a recurring annoyance. This past summer, the first one following the storm, foliage finally returned much of the city to life— but indiscriminately. Weeds were more voracious than usual, some becoming trash trees nurtured in sidewalk cracks, in mere weeks growing shoulder high. It's murder on a stroller, even their Congo Travel System is no match for it.

The Congo Travel System is a black stroller with small, loopy safari animals printed on beige on the inside. The feature that sold her on it was the black netting that hooks down in front, obscuring the Baby. It not only protects him from mosquitoes, which had also become especially aggressive, but she likes to think it also serves to veil him from the city. That morning they'd taken him for his six-month check up on the ninth floor of the still largely empty medical complex adjacent to Memorial Hospital. Blank rectangles of plywood were still screwed over smashed out windows, yards

190

of plastic sheeting still adorned the atrium, the concrete flooring on the pedestrian bridge to the elevators still revealed the abstract patterns of adhesive where the ruined carpet had been pulled up. She had just recently read a quote in the *Times-Picayune* from a spokesperson for the corporation that ran the hospital about why they waited four days to send the helicopters to save their own patients. "We didn't want to send assets into an unstable market." As they waited for the Baby's name to be called in the empty cheer of the pediatrician's office, they looked down through the picture windows at the roof of the parking garage where the help finally arrived, at the neighborhood where she grew up fanning out from Claiborne Avenue, at the napping asset in her arms.

Shreds of clouds stretch gauzily across the night sky, a half moon demures behind the scrim. It's several more blocks before they see another welcoming porch light. More smiles, more delight. "Trick or Treat!" Fists full of tiny chocolate bars the Mother eyes from behind the stroller. It's just like a year ago when they'd first come back and S. was a rock star, almost the only kid in the neighborhood in a city empty of children. People would hear his high-pitched voice or the slick rattle of his scooter and come to their doors with exclamations or just peer through the blinds. It was like science fiction, society thrown so far off kilter.

After another house of overzealous treat-giving, suddenly S.'s bright loot is all over the sidewalk and gutter of St. Roch Avenue, in between the scaly cypress knees of a tree slowly tearing up the concrete in front of the charred remains of a house. He clutches the tiny split-open bag and looks uncomprehending on the ground.

Just as he's about to wail, they hear Ms. Mouton call from across the street.

"Hey, what's going on over there?"

Ms. Mouton, a Creole lady and neighborhood fixture, is sitting on the stoop of her double shotgun with a Virgin of Guadalupe votive candle and bowl of Mary Janes and Coconut Long Boys.

The Mother explains the situation while crouched down searching the gutter with S. The baby is very asleep, lulled by the heat and motion. Ms. Mouton goes inside and comes back with a plastic orange bucket.

"Donated from Catholic Charities. I got a dozen of these back there."

Ms. Mouton had severe wind damage and gutted half of her house herself with her 78 year-old brother before getting on the wait list for Catholic Charities. The Mother and her husband had been on the crew that helped gut the rest.

"Look, honey, it's orange. It's perfect!"

"It's got words on it." S. points to the Home Depot logo. "Not even Halloween words."

"Look how much stuff you'll be able to hold." She quickly scoops up the loot and drops it in the bucket. "This is so much better."

The Mother asks about her house, remembers boxing up 20 years worth of Ms. Mouton's toiletries. Ms. Mouton says she can't get anyone to come hook up her hot water heater and bemoans the lack of trick-or-treaters, most of them not even wearing costumes, just demanding candy. She wants to see the Baby and the Mother lifts up the netting, nervous about what Ms. Mouton will say about his costume.

Ms. Mouton declares him a "fine, fine baby" and leans in to give his cheek a leathery stroke. "You got two fine boys," she says smiling.

"I know it." And she wheels them off.

The Mother tucks the broken bag into the other cup holder in the stroller and wishes she had something strong and cold to put in there instead. By the time they setout looking for another house, the bucket dangling jauntily from S.'s scooter handles, he's forgotten all about the bag.

The mother can't tell which houses are deliberately darkened to discourage trick-or-treaters (like she'd left their own, at the risk of encouraging burglars), or just unoccupied. They wander street after street with no strategy, S. scooting ahead, scouting for lights, the Mother withdrawing into herself, into the jagged rhythm of the Congo Travel System. A few blocks down she thinks she hears the group from the park and calls to S. to turn up ahead. S. enjoys a few more festive successes, amplified by the search. His bucket is just about topped off. She's exhausted, with damp armpits and the mosquito bites on the tops of her stroller-gripping hands are forming a Pangaea of welts she's helpless to stop.

As they near home, the resolute headlights of a National Guard Humvee from the unit that patrols the neighborhood advance around the corner. Its beaten armored sides and brawny desert colors always provoke both comfort and fear in the Mother. It stops and idles in front them. Taped on the back is a piece of typing paper with *Laissez Le Bon Temps Rouler* printed on it.

"Hey, kid, Happy Halloween!" one of the guardsmen yells from the backseat and extends his hand. She can almost hear the glistening crinkle of hard candy wrappers over the engine's rumble.

What is this, the Mother thinks, fucking Kabul?

S. walks his scooter up to the side of the Humvee to accept the treat, looking unbearably vulnerable with his tiny wheels and now crooked orange tail. He has a brief exchange with the guardsman holding out the candy.

"What'd he tell you?" she asks, waving and smiling as they drive off.

"He told me to be safe on this thing." S. dips the handle of his scooter.

Over the past year, scooting around the Bywater, he'd been snagged by the tangled nest of razor wire on Montegut and Royal left behind by the Oregon National Guard, he'd wiped out when he hit the carriage bolts sticking out of the pavement where the U.S. Postal Service removed one of the many doomed mailboxes in the area, swerved around piles of ever-appearing debris and glided over the painted messages on the streets: GOV. HELP and SEND FOOD & WATER.

It's time to go home. S.'s eyes are heavy and candy trails behind him out of his Home Depot bucket. Further down the poorly lit street, she thinks she sees three ghosts, of the old school bed-sheet-over-the head variety floating in the middle of the street. But she realizes that they are, in fact, three boys in ghetto gowns, huge white T-shirts that hang below their knees.

As if they had read her mind, as they approach one of them says, "Boo, bitch."

194

"Fuck off," she replies without thinking, some previous instinct bypassing the cautious motherly one she's been trying to encourage.

"You lucky you got your kids with you, bitch" says another and they continue walking towards the railroad tracks. One of them throws something, maybe a piece of candy S. has dropped, at a contractor's oversized F150 and the dull metallic ping disappears quickly in the empty street.

"Mom?" S. calls from up the street.

She can't see or think or say anything. S. doesn't seem to have heard. He's way ahead, eager to get home and paw through his loot. Her thoughts trot from the darkness back into jittery formation. Those kids. Must've been about twelve. Little dangerous assholes. Heading back to the wrecked fatherless streets across St. Claude.

She stops in front of the burned out Catholic church being fitfully restored on Dauphine Street, two by fours propping up the huge wooden doors blown down by the storm, re-positioned horizontally, as if against a siege. She peeks beneath the black netting to check on her sprawled sleeping baby, his defiant little fists clenched above his head, the lipstick marks like bright wounds. She jogs to catch up with her other son who was about to turn the corner and tries to shake the web of failure she'd stumbled into.

When she arrives home, the lights are still off but next door some unexpected Halloween jollity has erupted in their absence. S. disappears into fog billowing from their neighbors' window and into the street. At the last minute, the guys renovating the house next to theirs, a Creole cottage that fronts right onto the brick sidewalk, had gone nuts at Sam's Club, bought a fog machine, light-up black cats and witches and a CD of spooky-silly Halloween music.

"We got some! We actually got some trick-or-treaters. It was awesome!" Their ruddy, neatly bearded faces are glowing with Coors Light and goodwill as "One-eyed One-horned Flying Purple People Eater" plays, a corny old song even when the Mother was a kid.

"Dad!" Her husband, still in paint and plaster-splattered work clothes, accepts a hug from S. while trying not to spill the two sweating pints of beer in plastic go-cups.

"Here. It's still cold." He hands her one over their child's head.

She downs about half of it, relief drifting through her body, relief at his presence, at the cold beer, at their neighbors' awesome display.

Other folks from the block have gathered in their adult costumes, the forensic pathologist as Carrie, all slip dress and dried blood, his legs wobbling colt-like in stilettos, another couple in capes, she a sexy wench, he some kind of combative middle earth dweller. And now the guys themselves are getting ready to unplug the G-rated Halloween, trade out their baseball caps for leather and hit the clubs with the others. But before they leave, they want to take a picture of their neighbors, the family, who huddle close on the narrow sidewalk around the stroller, trying to fit into the frame.

In The Land Of Dreamy Diaspora
Leonard Earl Johnson

The second Christmas after Hurricanes Katrina and Rita destroyed New Orleans, the Sunset Limited pulled out of Union Station, on Loyola Avenue, and slipped past the wounded Louisiana Superdome. It left on time for Los Angeles, California, and points west. Since Amtrak service returned to The City FEMA Forgot, all trains have left on time. But they do not remain so very far down the road. By the time this one reached the Mississippi River it was running forty-five minutes late.

Once proud American passenger trains held right of way over approaching freighters. Now, humbled streamliners pull their passengers onto sidetracks and let the pig iron-laden freight trains roar past. By the time this one reached Houston it was five hours late. By the time it got to Los Angeles it was behind nearly a day. Fortunately, I was not going that far.

I was returning to the Hotel Evangeline, in Lafayette, Louisiana, where I have lived since The Storm. My trip back to New Orleans had been arranged by an old college friend I was to meet in a bar off Saint Charles Avenue.

The bar had clearly tried (with little success) to coax yuletide spirits from its Katrina-battered patrons. Above its polished mahogany dangled sparkling blue snowflakes and toy gray helicopters. The bartender had spent hours hanging each by invisible threads. The little choppers were lifting little refugees off little blue tarped roofs. There was one blue and white airplane with the U. S.

Presidential Seal painted around its nose and "FEMA" on its tail. From a bomb bay door, in its belly, confetti dropped whenever the bartender mashed a white button next to the cash register.

The bartender himself sported a red felt Santa's cap pulled down over long French black hair. White cotton sprinkled with glitter danced around his cap's rim and a silver bell dangled from its tapered tip. In spite of all this effort, the stars hung limp, and the bartender looked more weary than jolly.

My friend had arrived earlier in the day, aboard the train called The City of New Orleans. He had come from Chicago, Illinois, that broad-shouldered city on the other end of the Amtrak line, and had been riding— as a dedicated fan— with Arlo Guthrie, on his "City of New Orleans Tour."

Guthrie had made famous Steve Goodman's prophetic song, "Riding on The City of New Orleans," and was the son of America's legendary Depression Era folk singer, Woody Guthrie, who wrote many great songs, including, "This Land is Your Land," an idea we fear has passed us by.

The tour was designed to raise money to buy new instruments for musicians who had lost theirs in the hurricanes. They had stopped along the railroad route giving concerts and gathering funds. A few days earlier they had been gathering in Carbondale, Illinois, where my friend and I had gone to college. Tonight, we planned on going to Tipitina's and hearing Guthrie, with Willie Nelson, in the tour's last concert.

I spotted my friend at the end of the bar, overdressed and over-served. Temperatures had flirted with eighty degrees all day.

Yet, there he sat in a camel hair topcoat, wool suit and silk tie— a citizen of big cold shoulders detrained in the near tropics.

A mural behind the bar twinkled with tiny blue lights sprinkled over a snowy hillock full of white deer nibbling mistletoe berries dotted among evergreen boughs. The mistletoe berries were represented by tiny red lights.

"Mistletoe is poison," my friend was telling the bartender, "and the berries are white!"

A beer distributor from Saint Louis, Missouri was also behind the bar. He was passing out free samples of Red Wolf Beer. My friend took one and lifted it towards me. I moved down the bar and accepted the brew.

"Must be a Santa after all," my friend said to the largely empty room.

From a green felt poker table to the left of the French doors, an elderly couple I'd seen in this bar many times before The Storm looked up and smiled. No one was dealing and their cards were face up. I tipped my beer towards them.

They wore evening clothes, and his gold studs were set with diamonds that flashed back at the twinkling mural. She was ash blond and wearing a red-sequined gown decorated with jewelry that bespoke a high-maintenance lady. She bent her head and unzipped his tuxedo trousers. I nodded and said in stage whisper that she was an expensive date. He laughed and said, "How better to spend my FEMA money?" She laughed and slapped him playfully.

"Where is the "vice squad?" my friend asked in a real whisper.

"Saving patrons from the Feds, at some flooded brothel," I said.

My friend was in his cups and hanging his observations with Chicago bluntness. "Christmas in New Orleans is not like going over the river to grandmother's house, is it?"

"It's been a good system for hundreds of years," I said. "Tis better, we think, having vice cops protecting brothel patrons, and citizens in evening clothes entertaining themselves for free."

We looked again at the blond and my friend said, "Well, maybe not free, but a lot less than the cops are charging, I bet."

The beer distributor handed us two more Red Wolfs. He wanted to finish and leave. My friend asked, "Shouldn't you call this stuff Red Riding Hood?" None of us knew what he meant by that, but we laughed the laugh required of our respective stations.

In a few minutes, the beer distributor gave us two full six packs and said, "Please, friends, I gotta get to Baton Rouge and catch a plane back to Saint Louis."

The bartender said, "Let me put that on ice for you gentlemen."

I left to go to the restroom and my Chicago friend yanked a dangling blue snowflake from its tether. He bellowed at the bartender, "What fathead told you to hang blue snowflakes in this swamp?"

The bartender was startled and blurted back, "The corporate fatheads in Chicago who own this bar!" The bartender did not know he was talking to corporate fathead number-one.

The Saint Louis beer distributor smiled weakly and moved towards the double French doors, through which we saw a waiting limousine with rental license plates.

The man in the tuxedo fell off his chair. The woman in the red gown helped him to his feet and they stumbled outside holding onto an article of each other's clothing. They lunged into the limo and motioned for the Saint Louis beer man to join them. He shrugged and climbed in.

Coming out of the restroom, I put a quarter in a slot machine and watched the last of my FEMA money whirl away. I did not care. It was Christmastime and my friend was in Town to wine and dine us for three fat days - though our post Katrina tables might be thin and few. We had known each other since boyhood. He liked having, as he put it, "A creative bum for a friend." I liked having a rich one.

In a wastebasket, by the slot machines, I found a crumpled stack of little paper teddy bear Christmas tree ornaments. There were seven. Each had the name of someone lost in Hurricane Katrina or Rita. I picked one up and read the name printed across its stomach. Underneath was, "August 29, 2005." I smoothed them out and put them in my shirt pocket.

Back at the bar, we finished our beers in silence. The bartender, smarting from my friend's harsh words, glared and punched up "Blue Bayou," on the jukebox. Then he pushed the button releasing confetti into our empty glasses. He still did not know he was glaring at his boss.

We stood to leave, and I told the bartender to keep the remaining Red Wolfs. My friend gave him a one hundred dollar bill and his business card. "Tell those fatheads in Chicago to go jump in Lake Michigan," he said. "New Orleans is a swamp, not a snowy wonderland."

Outside, he gaped at the empty curb. "Where the hell's my driver?" he said, throwing his hands in the air.

I said, "Forget it, let's walk."

He slipped out of his topcoat and handed it to a bewildered man in dirty blue jeans and a black T-shirt that read in white lettering: "Be a New Orleanian Wherever You Are".

We moved along debris-littered streets towards Tipitina's. I took the paper teddy bears from my pocket. My friend held one up to the street light and said, "Ah, Christ, what am I supposed to do about this?" Then he handed it to a couple also walking towards Tip's.

"Let's distribute them like hand bills," he said, and we walked to Tip's singing, "We three kings of Orient are . . ."

When someone asked, "Where is your other king?" we handed them a paper teddy bear. "Bearing gifts we traveled so far..."

ONE HOUR TURN-AROUND ON MARDI GRAS PHOTOS

Jason Berry

Ash Wednesday in the holy city of New Orleans. Carnival debris chokes the gutters. Inside Walgreens, a line of people, many with darkened foreheads from Catholic Mass, are backed up, waiting to purchase their photographs.

At the front of the line, an African-American lady is explaining to the cashier: "It is five stubs, for three people. I'm paying for all three."

"Stop it!" snaps her teenage daughter, pinching the arm of little brother, a button of a boy in fine blue suit.

A howl of terror rises from the boy.

The mother turns to the sister with a look of ferocity that would make Donald Rumsfeld freeze: "You apologize to your brother and *stop* all this commotion carry'n-on!"

Leon's lips tighten, the chin shakes.

"*Sorry,*" sulks the sister, thin as a reed in Gap jeans and Hornets jersey. Sister gazes at the ice cream cooler, rear left of the photo desk.

"And no sass outta *you,* young Mistah!" glowers the mother.

Leon swallows, manfully.

His mother returns to the transaction at hand.

Sister releases a bullet of tongue at Leon, then pulls it in as if landing a trout.

Leon glares back.

Behind them, a voice ragged from cigarettes and God-knows-what, opens on a B-flat hum: "This is a waste. Tony can't take a picture." The words belong to a twentysomething Goth with a neck of floral tattoos, nose rings, eyebrow rings, black jeans, black shirt.

"Anyone can take a picture, even Bush," snorts his galpal, of roughly equivalent age, sheathed in velvet turquoise jeans, pink lamé coat and matching pink hair. She stands, sword straight, to the Goth's craggy slump.

Leon stares at them, his lips forming the shape of an egg.

"All-a-times Tony's finger smudged the lens," growls the Goth.

"*Put it to sleep*," his woman simmers.

At the front of the line, Leon's mother is reviewing matters with the young woman cashier. "That's mine, that's the other one, and my brother…yes, that would be his. You should have one, no, two others."

"Did they lose mine?" whimpers Leon, burrowing next to his mother.

"Shush, Leon," says the older sister.

The boy makes a fist.

Sister does tongue-stabs toward Leon -- in-and-out, in-and-out -- nebulously obscene acts to the boy.

Folding his arms, Leon raises his chin.

"….because Tony *never had time*," comes the end-fragment from galpal to the Goth. Her spiked hair and pink radiance rivet the gaze of Leon's big sister.

"All I ever hear," retorts her Goth, "is Tony wants ice, Tony wants a chili dog, Tony wants, Tony wants, Tony wants. I never saw

Tony stand in will-call. What about that? I never saw him once push a basket at Winn-Dixie. I bet you Tony hadn't been in Winn-Dixie since, what, back when they had Ninja-Turtles. Myself, how many times did *I* stand in will-call?"

"Tony *pays*," she reports, rolling her eyes.

"*I want mine!*" declares Leon.

"Hold on," says the mother, producing an ATM card for the cashier.

Leon takes the small packages with the photographs from his mother.

His sister sweeps the photo-packs out of Leon's hands and pries open the envelope on top.

"Give it over!" squeals the boy.

"Your uncle took these," the sister says teasingly, holding negatives up to the light, gazing into a new, hidden universe. "All these Mardi Gras parades!" she sings.

Leon lunges, the sister pivots, gripping photo-packs like grapes to a fox.

Another wail rises from Leon.

The Goth cringes. His girlfriend looks at her shoes.

"*Give Leon his,*" orders the mother, waiting for the receipt.

The sister hands the stack of photo-packs to Leon and drifts toward the cosmetics display.

Greedily, Leon opens the photo-pack.

"Tony don't add anti-freeze, Tony don't change oil," mutters the Goth. "Things a qualified person knows, when you got a vehicle. What happens to a dude like dat? Pff. Somebody open a window.*"

In a sudden gesture of intimacy, the girlfriend with pink spiked hair touches the Goth on the back of his neck, tamping her fingers down on his tattooed flower bed to lower the emotional temperature.

He breaks a crooked smile.

"That's one I took!" cries Leon, rifling through the pictures: "That's one I took! She's smiling and she got no teeth."

The sister looks up. "No teeth?"

"Awright, you young Mister," broods the mother, folding the receipt into her purse.

"I know who lost their teeth," says the sister.

Leon, exultant: "I gotta picture of the teeth too! Settin' up top the bureau!"

"*Teeth?*" queries the mother, reaching for the image.

"Hah!" cries Leon, bolting toward the magazines.

"*Leon,*" commands the mother, right hand clamping on his shoulder, terminating his sprint in the tracks. "What kind of picture is this?"

"Dentures," yawns the sister. "T-Anne before Zulu."

"Buy me an ice cream," pleads Leon.

As the woman and her children retreat to the frozen foods, the Goth and his gal move irritably to the head of the line. The Goth presents his photo-pack stub to the cash register.

"Tony's got the *car*," she says.

"Tradeoffs," grumbles the Goth.

"Uh, yeh-*uhhh.*"

Something is happening behind the cashier's table.

The young woman collecting the film and disposable cameras scans the computer records, which come up blank. She whispers to the store manager, his attention diverted by fill orders in the long line. The manager, a Hindu, takes the photo-pack stub the

Goth has handed the clerk, studies it for an eternity of seconds, and then with doleful eyes, returns it to the Goth.

"I am sorry," says the manager. "We cannot help you at this Walgreens, sir. This ticket is for another one of our stores."

The Goth scratches his neck. "Which Walgreens you talkin' about?"

"I'm afraid I don't know, sir. The stubs are similar but you see, it doesn't have the name of the branch. Is there another store you patronize?'

"I'm not big on patronizin'."

"Are you the person who dropped the film off?"

"Ah, that was a frienda ours. Tony. He's out in the parking lot."

"Well, I think Tony made a mistake," says the manager with a tone of consolation. "I'm sorry we are unable to fill the order for you at this Walgreens. You could call the other branches but I'm sure you'll find your pictures. Please try us again, sir."

"That's right." The Goth's shoulders hunch. Lips pursed, he pushes off, his hands stuffed in his pockets.

"Must be Walgreens on Tchoupitoulas," says the girlfriend.

"Tony been sitting out there this whole time. Man don't have any idea about *reality* – you hear what I'm saying?"

She yawns. "We ain't taking no streetcar."

A City For A River
Justin Burnell

Sugar Park is nearly empty. It's the type of place people don't go out of their way to visit, a neighborhood bar. There's a camera above the door. At night you have to be buzzed in by the bartender. James is already posted at the corner of the bar with a PBR in front of him. He's staring at the wall-mounted TV at the opposite end of the room.

"Hey."

"Hey." He turns to face me, holding out his hand. We shake; I sit down and order a beer.

"Where's your girl?" James smirks at me. The bartender brings me a can of PBR from a blue portable ice chest.

"She's running late. Said she'd be here in an hour or so." I take a drink of beer. It's hot enough outside that it only tastes cold, and that's enough.

"She doesn't have to come out here. It's a drive from Uptown. I don't want her to think that I would be offended."

"I doubt she's worried about offending you." I met Shelia in the Uptown restaurant she waits tables at, and had given her my phone number after giving her a hard time for being a shitty waitress. She called and we went out for drinks almost two months ago. She's a nice enough girl, but I wouldn't say I'm committed to a relationship with her. "Why are you such a dick about her anyway?"

"I don't know," He said looking up at the television. The Cubs are playing. Top of the fourth. No score. "I mean, come on, you've got to wonder about a girl who runs around in a pair of Tulane sweat-shorts."

"Yeah," I laugh, "but it's more play than you get."

"Whatever."

"Right." He gnaws at the dead skin on his middle finger.

"Too much work. It's never easy, you know." He says, the end of his finger still between his teeth.

James and I drink quietly, half watching the game, half listening to the conversations around us. It's cool and decently lit, but the naked rafters and silver air-conditioning tubes above remind you where you are. The beer is cold and that's still its only attraction. A short guy with a shaved head, wearing a T-shirt with the sleeves and most of the side cut off is laughing, loudly telling a kid with dreadlocks at least a foot long, that octopi are intelligent creatures. He slams his beer on the bar, exclaiming that people look down on invertebrates. According to him scientists found that octopi can open and close mason jars. Dreadlocks nods in agreement. I smile over to James. He winces at the conversation. The bartender is asking some one with a neck tattoo when Potato is going to get his van fixed and come back. He looks over at us. We order two more beers. I pay for the round.

James takes a drink of beer. "You got a smoke?" He asks, his hand reaching for the pack in front of me.

"Sure. You smoke a lot for someone who doesn't."

"I'm drinking," he says, taking the lighter off the bar. "I smoke when I drink."

"You could buy a pack." He shrugs handing back the lighter. He picks up his beer, pauses and takes a long drink. I light a cigarette for myself. The Cubs are up. One nothing. Bottom of the fifth. The bartender lights a cigarette and sits down to watch the game. A thousand miles away from Wrigley Field, this city is filled with lifelong Cubs fans. With no local team, people take what basic cable gives them.

"How's the house?" James asks, can half way to his mouth, held in abeyance as he watches the batter swing.

"It's fine. Still cheap." The batter strikes out. Dreadlocks leaves. The bald kid in the sack of a shirt orders a beer. James looks over at me.

"And the roommates?" He smiles.

"Fuck them. I need to move out. I mean, it's not that I hate them. They're just dirty and young." Defining them as young makes me feel old, but it also gives me a satisfying sense of passage.

James cringes as the Mets score with two men on base. "There are some places around here for rent."

"Yeah, I've seen a few. I'll get back here. I just don't have any money right now." I finish my beer. "Speaking of which, think you can get the next round?"

"I've got a few beers in my bag. Let's go out to the wharf."

"That one you told me about?" James doesn't answer, I look up and watch as the Mets score on a single. He makes a face of disapproval and nods his head.

"Yeah, at the bottom of Piety," he says, turning away from the game.

I nod toward the TV and ask, "Aren't you watching this?"

"Cubs are giving it up," he says as they close out the inning. An old black man stands next to me at the end of the bar, trying to get the bartender's attention. He was posted at a video poker machine when I walked in, I wonder if, and how much, he won.

The bartender saunters over to him, slight annoyance showing in his face. He orders a cup of ice.

"I should wait on Shelia. She'll be here soon. I can start a tab, and borrow money when she gets here." I wonder how many drinks she had bought me since I met her.

"Sure, man, whatever you want to do." He lifts his eyes back to the game. At some point the sack-shirt guy was replaced by a sloppy-looking girl with short blonde hair, and a semi-chubby, but not unattractive chick with black hair that hung just below her ear. She keeps running her fingers around her ear making sure her hair is still in place. She laughs at something the blonde says. She has a cute smile. "The Cubs tied it." James breaks in, looks at the girls, and smirks at me. "Won't Shelia be here soon?"

"Yeah, why?"

"Just asking."

"Don't be a dick." Sometimes James was funny, and other times he just managed to piss me off. "She's on her way by now."

James grabs my pack off the bar, taking a cigarette for himself, then offers one to me. I light the cigarette and take a drag slowly. The girls laugh. I think about the last time I fucked Shelia, and smile toward them. James looks pleased as the Cubs end the inning up by three. "I'm not telling you to leave but I've seen you do worse to better."

"Yeah," I take another long drag, realizing that I need another beer. "But I don't want to pull shit like that anymore." I say this with a slight hope that it's true. I know I want to stop being so fucking selfish, but I feel like I know it more in theory than anything else.

"How long did Lisa wait at that restaurant?" James laughs at the same time as the girls across the bar giggle loudly.

"That was a long time ago." I want to remove myself from all sins committed before the storm. As if I get to start over.

"No. No. Weren't you plastered at the fucking Dervish of all places. No. That was when you were up all night with that cokehead bartender. The tall bald one." He's gripping his knee to brace himself. His head bent down, laughing hard with white spit on the edges of his lips, a thin string of saliva stretched between them. I flex my jaw, and turn my head away. I stare back at the television, watching James through the corner of my eye. He settles down a little, and turns his attention back to the game. I pick up the empty can and tilt it back anyway. James timidly reaches for the pack that sits between our arms. I don't flinch. He lights a cigarette, and looks down at his own empty can. I order another beer.

"Zambrano is having a good year despite all the injury talk," he says softly enough that it could be to himself.

"Yeah." I pick up my new beer, and feel a little stupid. "He's won nine now?"

"If he wins this one." There was another lull. I sit and drink the beer that I don't have the money to pay for. I did do an excessive amount of coke with that bartender. His name was Devin, Darren or something. All he could talk about was bartending. Stories about stupid bartenders, and crazy drunks. All service industry stories start to blur after awhile. He did let me do a lot of blow. He kept saying he had a "sweet-tooth ache." He'd stretch back the corner of his mouth and try to cleanly rap a knuckle on the tooth. He'd stop talking, and I'd look up and see him violently striking at the inside of his mouth. Thinking about that tooth always made me feel a little better.

"It was three hours." I say.

"Three hours is a long time." His laugh is small and controlled. The girls across the bar are getting up to leave. I watch them, keeping my grin pointed at the cute one.

"Yeah, it was our anniversary. She was at the Court of Two Sisters." I laugh. The girls leave without looking toward us. "You still want to go?"

"What about your girl?" James sounds surprised and sincere. For a second I almost want to spit on him. "She'll be pissed."

"Yeah, but that's all tomorrow." I say standing up.

We walk out of the bar into the weighty night-heat and unlock our bikes. James shoulders his bag, swings his leg over the bike seat, and takes off. It's still hot enough to sweat, but Piety is only about five blocks away, and biking creates enough breeze to compensate for its effort. The street's vacant, lined with old, shitty cars. Quiet shotgun doubles stand peacefully together against a bright starless sky. Occasionally I can hear a TV or parts of a conversation through a closed metal security door, the wooden door left open to let in the night air, the street noise mingling unopposed with the sounds of nightly routines. A few blocks from Piety thin two black men are talking to a couple sitting on a stoop. The standing men are laughing, one leans over to set down his beer. The couple is smiling back at them. They look up at us. Their conversation quiets, and I nod my head in greeting. One raises his hand. The woman nods. One of the standing men mumbles "all right". They seem unsure about us. Behind us I can hear their voices grow and echo off the houses.

We stop to lock up our bikes to a fence next to a large white satellite dish. James points to a cement wall with a simple wrought iron latter attached to it. "It's over this." The wall hid train tracks and an unkempt field. The tall, weedy grass scratches and tickles my legs. I slap my caves, and claw at the burs and seedpods stuck in my leg hair. I follow James, walking parallel to the tracks as looking for a break in the razor-wired fence. He turns, walking backward, "There's a place where the fence fell up here."

The fence hadn't fallen. The cement had shifted, sliding down the bank, taking the fence with it. It's still securely attached to the concrete, but now it's flat against the bank. The razor wire barred the way at mid-leg height. It was crimped in places, losing some of its original coiled form. It reflects the streetlights behind us, glimmering with battlefield amputations. I carefully raise one leg, placing it between two widely spaced coils. In the midst of the razor wire, between here and there I look across the river; lighted buildings illuminate the opposite bank. Between the coils, neutral and indifferent. Separate from the field, but not on solid ground. Moribund and wide-eyed I step out on to a broken slab of cement, leaving a city to stand at the edge of a river.

The breeze is cool on my back as we walk over the concrete terrain eyeing the blackened beams, lit by the reflection of city lights off the river. Some leaned, curled by fire and time, while others still support corners of slate plateaus. Most of the wharf connected to land was slanted and sliding into the bank of the river. The parts farther out rose up from the river to rest on beams ready to give up the fight. James stops, looks over the glowing and fragmented sweep, and heads out toward a high peak over the river.

The Orange Street wharf had burned down twice and has now been left to slowly sink into the river. James had told me he found it back in the curfew days, while looking for a place to hang out at night. Burned timbers still stood amid the rolling slabs of concrete. As the support beams had buckled with the fire, thousands of pounds of flat grey concrete had fallen but not broken. A man poured vista of muted hills, valleys, and jutting cliffs. It's as if the fire had melted the entire structure as one piece, cooling wrinkled and deformed like plastic.

"I think it's still sinking. Every time I come back parts look lower." James had sat down, letting his legs dangle off an edge still lofted in the air by a half-burned pillar. I put my hand down to brace myself; the concrete matched the cool river breeze. Bending down to sit, I look down at the water below us, about a ten or twelve foot drop, the jagged, fallen section probably just under the surface.

"You've never seen a piece like this fall, right?" I ask, still eyeing the black water.

"No, seems like they held up pretty well. All of it'll fall though, it's just a matter of years." James grips the edge by his legs; head turned looking out over the river. "Probably won't be tonight. Get a beer out of my bag." Twisting back, I lay half my chest against the chill pavement to reach the bag behind us. I push the bag, nudging it onto his back, roll over, and let the concrete absorb my body heat. It's a hot, clear night. The sky is a starless, pallid-black city sky.

James says something. I raise my head off the incline and see a beer held over my legs. Sitting up, I take the beer, still PBR, and drink. The city lights from the West Bank are reflected, rippling in the meandering current, answering the bank sky. No one ever mentions how the sky looked framed by powerless buildings. Maybe the stars don't shine on a dead city. Above the river, the city sparkles quietly, stories of lit windows, rows leading down into the water, shining vigilantly above, wavering and liquid below.

"I like the city better from out here."

"Yeah. It makes you forget. It's peaceful." James' voice doesn't resonate. The silence soaks up noise, muffling intonation and accent. He stares out across the river, raising his can to drink in an unconscious rhythm. His face is deadpan. It's hard to tell what, if anything, his words meant. I take out two cigarettes, and offer him one. He hands me a beer in response. A light in a window flicks off. Third floor, fifth from the right.

James turns, his face contorted in thought. "Did you pay for that last beer?"

"Shit, I forgot." I laugh. "Guess I thought I didn't have to worry about it because Shelia was coming." Being in bad standing isn't the best feeling, but I don't want to go all the back just to pay for a beer. Not that I have the money anyway.

"You want to go back? I've got a few bucks if you don't." He should have just bought the round in the first place.

"I doubt it'll be a big deal. I'll pay next time I'm there." I flick my cigarette. It arches high, landing in the water with a clipped hiss. "I'd be surprised if they even remember."

James laughs, pats my back, and says, "Give me another beer, will you." I light another cigarette, inhale deeply; reach behind him grabbing another a beer. From one long drink to another. Over the river in front of us, and across the barbed wire behind, a

221

city half full, still moving at an amble. The water under my feet is black and still. The moisture climbs into the air, weighing the heat against my body, clinging to my shoulders, looking for a free ride. It saps my strength. The end of my cigarette is wet against my lips. The aluminum can warm in my hand, I taste the salt in my beer. The river stench is dirty and cool in my nose. Lakeside, riverside, and a thousand canals: a city surrounded by water with no ocean. The smell of brackish air hangs at the edges, fills my lungs with beach air, promising leisure, peace, the roar of a tidal surge. The city lights burn, making James a silhouette next to me. His head tilts back to finish his beer. His arm rises back in a practiced fluid motion, bringing the can behind his head. His body twists slightly, arm coming down fast in black streak. The can wobbles helplessly in the air, dimly reflecting the distant lights, falling into the water with a small noise.

Hot White Cum
Bill Lavender

It was three years Before Katrina (BK) that R started fucking her husband's best friend. He, R's husband, we'll call him S, had gotten a job with an architectural firm in Santa Cruz and they'd moved out there from New Orleans. In a way, they said, they were always more California than New Orleans anyway.

But they missed their good friends U and V. S and U had worked together at the firm in New Orleans, and the foursome were well known at the fancy restaurants in the Quarter. They used to take the kitchen table at August and be served by the chef without ever looking at a menu.

But California was good to R and S, with S knocking down mid-six figures and R soon landing a gig utilizing ("finally") her writing skills, scooping investment tips for a trade magazine. And so in what was really a very short time, just 9 months or so, they were ready to buy their very own California condo.

They even bought a wine cooler— nothing fancy, just a regular fridge with all the shelves taken out and a special thermostat to keep it exactly 56 degrees at all times and the freezer a little colder for beer. And they filled the fridge up with nice wines from California and France and they put little labels on each bottle's neck to they could see them easily from the front without having to pull them out.

They came back to New Orleans now and then and got together with U and V and S and U would smoke cigars and drink single malts at the hotel bars.

Then one day R got a call and had to come back suddenly because her mother was sick. She and I went out to eat that night. She called up U and V to let them know, but V was busy and U had to come meet us alone.

We went to dinner and then to my neighborhood bar and after a while I was talking to some friends and lost sight of them. When I looked around I found them over at the end of the bar making out.

I went home by myself and was sound asleep at five a.m. when she came knocking on the window. I asked her if she fucked him.

"No, by the grace of god, I didn't fuck him. He couldn't get it up. No I didn't fuck him, thank god, and why would I even want to? You know how quick S gets a hard-on? Why would I want to fuck some guy who can't get it up, for fuck's sake? He could barely get it up for a blow job."

She emailed me as soon as she got back to Santa Cruz saying she was done with that foolishness and it would never happen again. But of course you already know that it did, that she kept coming back to New Orleans on business or sometimes on "business" and before she knew it— almost like she slipped into it unawares— they were fucking full on, every time she can get away, and she's telling me about it sometimes and sometimes not.

Meanwhile the foursome continued their restaurant, cigar, and single malt hunt unabated, with expensive drinks and gossip from the office, and all of them making enough money that they could literally fly into one place or another just for dinner. And R and U got into playing footsy under the table while S and V gushed over the soup or copping feels in the hallway when no one was looking, and S and V never suspect a thing because all four of them were quite close and always hugging and kissing and flirting and just having a great time getting drunk.

I know that outsiders to a situation like this always want to say that the cuckolds knew all along, that they were in denial or just playing along or even watching out of the corner of their prurient eyes, but in this case S and V didn't know a thing. They truly believed they were all four good friends and good friends kiss and flirt, and it wasn't like R wasn't fucking S anymore or U V; in fact the only ones who weren't fucking were S and V and— who knows?— even they might have gotten a little amorous after scotches one night while R and U were dancing. But it didn't go any farther than that and as the months and as the years went by R and U got more and more adept at the deception and instead of S and V starting to notice the millions of hints they became inured to them and so suspected less and less even as R and U were doing more and more.

R talked to me a great deal about it at the beginning, but after a while it lost that delicious badness that had set her heart aflutter. She talked about it like she talked about anything else, not with an air of salacious gossip but more in the line of reporting her itinerary, explaining why her separate commitments to S and U and V were preventing her from attending this or that party or dinner or evening at the bar. It was almost like she had two husbands. She and U started coming up with ways to up the risk factor: lamer and lamer excuses, squeezing dates into shorter and shorter intervals, blow jobs in the bathroom, fucking in the car, risking discovery just to get their hearts pounding.

The crowning example of this being the decision to move back to New Orleans.

She sat down with S in Santa Cruz and told him.

"My life's going nowhere here; I miss the French Quarter. I miss Mardi Gras. I miss the kitchen table at August. My mother's getting older and she's going to need help soon. My sister's there. We don't really have any friends out here. I can do my job from anywhere. In fact, I can tide us over while you get started. And you, for that matter, could use a change yourself. Don't you think it's time you started your own firm? I'll bet U would come work for you in a heartbeat?"

In the end she won him over by making him think that maybe her malaise when she was with him now might be solved by bringing her back, that maybe the relationship would find new life back in the old place. So they packed up the truck and the dog and sold the condo— on which they made the customary California quarter million— and came on back to New Orleans. They got an apartment by Bayou St. John and pretty soon found a little house looking out onto the water and got an offer accepted under three fifty, and S set about designing, worrying how to fit the jacuzzi and an office for him and an office for her and a little pool in the back— a really efficient use of the small space, simple and elegant— and he looked around for a contractor and found a carpenter to get it started and a foundation crew to start the addition in the back.

S had, of course, his work to consider too and, just like R had predicted, U started working for him right away, at first just helping out on some projects because S couldn't handle it all, finally quitting the firm and coming on full time. They started talking about the possibility of a partnership.

Then came a thing called Katrina.

The two couples saw it coming and talked it over and decided to evacuate together in R's SUV. R and S and U and V, along with V's mom. The five of them took off for anyplace out of here when the swirl approached on the map. They went to Texas, little knowing they'd be there two months. They wound up with friends in Plano. Like the rest of us, they hunkered down in strange living rooms and watched CNN for images of their neighborhood. When the helicopter hovered over their house on the bayou, they pointed and whooped and screamed.

But, Katrina or no, there was still work to be done, a living to be made. S and U and what they were starting to think of as their fledgling firm would fly off to Portland or Savannah or Denver or New York for meetings, leaving R and V and V's mom at their temporary home in Plano. R could work from her Blackberry, but she tried to relax some too, and she and V began to get quite close; they went shopping together, bought boots together. R showed me pictures afterwards and begged me to note the cowboy motif.

"Watch," she said, leafing through the prints, "you'll see the cowboy stuff more and more." And sure enough I did. First just R in boots, then V too. Then finally all five of them in boots and ten-gallon hats. I told her she was the world's worst photographer (and she was, heads cut off, frame out of level, too dark, too bright, you name it). "Shut up," she said.

I asked her how it was living with U and V and V's mom.

"Oh it's been great. We've just become a fivesome. V and I've been having a great time, and I love her mom too."

And U?

"Well, it's just a thing, you know. I love him to death. That's all I can say. I mean, it feels bad sometimes, but then it feels so good. We're trying to be discrete, but sometimes there's a little too much temptation. S and V like to go to bed early, you know, so U and I get left drinking wine by the pool lots of nights, if you know what I mean. Mmmm, that pool. I don't know what we're going to do. I don't know. I guess it's time I had a talk with S."

When they came back to the city they threw the fridge-full of expensive wine away unopened. There was no way it could have survived two months without electricity. And R began her conversation with her husband, telling him the truth, about how she was feeling unfulfilled in their relationship and she just didn't know how it was going to turn out. She even floated the D-word, just to test the water.

S didn't say much to her, but he had a long talk with U next day at work, and U told her all about it a couple of days later in bed. "He's worried," said U, "that you might be seeing someone." They raised their eyebrows in unison. He dropped his head and languidly licked her nipple. "He's confused and upset," he smacked, "really upset, but refusing to show it in front of you." He paused to suck hard for a moment, and then let go. "I feel bad. I need to do something for him. I should take him camping or something, some kind of guy thing."

"What are you talking about?" she blurted. "You're his best friend. You're the one he talks about it to, the only one. You have

230

nothing to feel guilty about. Nothing at all. You're there when he needs you. What more could he ask?"

"I guess you're right," he sighed. "There isn't much more to be done."

He let go of her tit and lay back on the pillow, and she went to work on his.

It only took about a month of R's whining about self-fulfillment to get S moved out of the apartment and into his studio. Luckily the place he had rented for his office in the Quarter had enough room for him to live comfortably. I went down and saw it one evening soon after he moved in.

Sweet little place, ancient wood floors and exposed brick walls, high ceilings, everything you would want in a French Quarter pad. The studio was properly architectural, not a pin out of place, nothing but a table on sawhorses, a laptop, and one of those big photo-quality ink-jet printers. The chair looked like a design drawing for a chair, so skeletal it was.

He and I went out for a drink and I asked him how he was.

"I'm ok," he said. "I'm really not worried about me. It's R that has the problem, you know. I'm worried about her. She's a deer in the headlights, you know? She doesn't make any sense. I ask her how she's doing and she just says 'oh, well, ok, I guess, I don't know.' I don't know what to do. I just know she's unhappy. And I feel bad, like it's my fault"

We poured down more than a few single malts that night. Then he went home to his lonely bed. I felt wretched, sullied, being part of it.

***

A few days later R comes barging into my living room without knocking, her arms laden with Saks bags. ("Saks," she said once on her blog, "is where the pulchritude shop.") She dropped them on the floor, kicked off her shoes, and began to disrobe. When she got down to bra and panties she started pulling stuff out of the bags and gradually appeared before me in a mini-skirt, go-go boots, and fishnets, with a sequined top.

"What do you think?" she said.

I told her it looked good, though in truth her fifty-year-old thighs were a little big for the skirt. I asked her what the occasion was.

"Well," she got down to business, "U's going to Savannah this weekend to meet with a big client, and they're having a cocktail party on a yacht in the river Saturday night. I told S I was going to Texas to see Robin. We're taking separate flights to Atlanta but then transferring to the same flight from there to Savannah. I'm really excited— never been to Savannah."

I wondered if S might not suspect something, with the two of them leaving on the same weekend.

"No way," she said. "I've had this trip planned for months. It's all working out."

Actually she was right. He didn't suspect a thing. Still it came as no surprise to me when my phone rang Monday morning and it was S saying:

"So I got an email this morning from some contractor in Savannah saying he'd really like to work with us, but then at the end he says he really enjoyed meeting U and R at the party last night. Is this true? Did R sneak up there with U? Are they having an affair or something?"

Though my silence told him more than anything else, in the end I fessed up. It felt good to be out of the deception, but when I heard his voice quaver I knew the depth of the betrayal and I just wanted to get off the phone.

All the rest is pretty predictable. Rage turning into tears and back again. Even R, a person I am wont to classify as devoid of affect, cried a couple of times. V was particularly shitty to her, one day, and she came crying to me, incredulous. "How could she be so cruel and thoughtless?" she said, without a hint of irony.

U went back to the firm, of course, and also, after a month of yammering and basically saying whatever R wanted to hear, back to V. S started spending more and more time in the air, flitting to Portland and Savannah and San Francisco and DC. He went through three girlfriends in three months before settling with number four, in Portland.

We had a party for R down on the bayou one night, and she burned U in effigy.

"You know what the worst thing about this is," she confided to me that night. "It's the no-sex. I mean, why did I go through all this except for the sex. Where's *my* hot white cum?"

She found some, shortly thereafter, inside a 25 year-old coke dealer she met at Cosimo's, then hooked up in a more serious way with a guy that lived down the street. She called him "the pole," and it wasn't a reference to his nationality. I would see her leaving his house at 7 a.m. when I was walking the dog. Then one morning I saw her coming out... but it wasn't her. It was a friend of hers, one of her bar-hopping buddies. I asked her about it the next time I saw her.

"Oh, the pole. He's the pole, you know? What else can I say? He wasn't all I hoped he would be."

I pressed the matter.

"What do you care anyway? Why are you always lurking around in my shit, making me out to be so horrible? I'm trying to understand myself. Trying to be a better person. That's all. Oh, fuck off anyway."

I didn't say anything.

"Fuck off."

HOPELESS
Karissa Kary

James heard the alarms and the police sirens. It was time to go home. He saw a cigarette burning on the ground. It looked new. He picked it up and took a few drags before heading back home to his wife. She would complain to him about the leaking ceiling in his house in Treme.

He looked around Jackson Square slowly. It was getting dark and he needed to get home soon. Before the storm James had been a street musician, but he hadn't felt like singing since then. He had started selling Mardi Gras beads to get by.

"Gotta remember the po-pos on Royal. They don't want to see you approaching the tourists. Can't even ask the people if they have some change. Not like I'm begging, I'm giving them some beads. Gotta remember the po-pos on Royal."

As James scoped out bead-needing walkers, the po-pos were indeed on Royal. What he didn't know is that they had more than his bead antics to worry about.

On Royal was Officer Lucas who had already had a full day. Two abuse calls, three street harassments, one driving violation (the guy had almost run him over, for Christ's sake) and now this. Someone had broken into a gallery. Or at least it looked that way. Alarm blaring, broken glass, an open gate. He had been driving back to the precinct office, just a few blocks away, to drop off his paperwork before going home. He had his window rolled down and had heard the siren go off, a block away at the most. He arrived at the gallery, saw the broken glass on the side of the building and the lights flashing inside. Officer Lucas called for backup, but he doubted the thieves were there anymore. The gate was swinging out, and it had taken him several minutes to get to the gallery with traffic. When he called, he told them there had been a robbery and to be on the lookout for anyone carrying "art."

The patrol team took over the case as they had been following a series of robberies in the area. He signed over the case paperwork and left. Two weeks later Officer Lucas would get a report in his inbox about the specifics, two large canvasses stolen and one print. He didn't know but the print was one of his favorites, a woman on a small rock surrounded by rising water. In the print the woman is playing a handheld harp and she is blindfolded. Will the waters envelope her or will they recede?

The name of the picture and the name of the woman in the picture is Hope.

APOCALYPSE ANGELS
Kelly Gartman

I often go out drinking at night and then drive toward Lake
Pontchartrain, out to Gentilly and Lakeview, near the shore where
people fish under shade trees during the day and the Orleans Levee
Board building squats stonily with its back to the city. I drink in
dark bars downtown and then I drive around, looking at the houses
and abandoned shops on Elysian Fields Avenue. I drive down
Burbank Street, past the house where my ex used to live. The door
has been hanging open for nearly two years now. There's nothing
inside but mold, guck, exposed beams, rodents and bugs, and a few
sun-bleached and sodden remnants of his life: pieces of a finger
painting made while he was on LSD, a forlorn voodoo doll, some
loose, faded Mardi Gras medallions that fell from his dad's chain
mail costume. The smell of waterlogged wood and mold still hangs
in the air here despite the constant breeze off the water.

Someone has spray painted KEEP OUT FEMA! on a piece
of sheet metal and propped it up against a hollow, stone-faced one-
story near the corner of Prentiss Avenue and Elysian Fields. A trailer
is parked in the front yard near a stone statue of a woman holding
flowers. The statue is covered in green algae and the windows of
the house are all busted. Tall weeds have taken over the front yard.
There isn't room in a trailer for a proper lawn mower, and if one is
left out at night, it won't be there in the morning. There are scores
of homes like this one, whole neighborhoods that drown in the
darkness over and over again every evening, a white trailer here and

there acting as a fragile bastion against the squatters, drug dealers and copper looters. I drive in the dark, alone, my tires thudding against broken pavement. I smoke and I drive in silence, sweating. Listening.

Last night, as I passed under the green light at Elysian Fields and Humanity Street, my car slammed into what felt like a concrete wall, then skidded into the cement post under the overpass. Dazed, I got out and looked around. Dirty white feathers longer than yardsticks poked out from under the car. I bent down to look. He was an older one, probably a few thousand years or more. Silver-grey hair hung in frail tendrils from his alabaster scalp. My tire was flat. I guess he grabbed it to keep the car from rolling over him at the last moment, then threw my car to the side.

They let their fingernails grow long, sharp and thick as butcher blades when they get bad off like this. The nails can puncture most anything, even steel. I saw one hanging by his fingernails off the Huey P. Long bridge undercarriage early one morning about a month ago. I guess he changed his mind in mid-plummet and grabbed for the beams. His nails pierced straight through. He hung there in terrific pain, his long, opaque nails splintering, stuck through the rusted steel. I didn't know what to do. I kept driving.

I bent down and hooked my arms under his, pulled him out and propped him up against the passenger door. Reddish purple blood plopped in half-dollar-size drips onto his gown. The material slowly changed from grey to white to silver to blue, then back again. His legs looked busted up and his dirty toes were longer than my fingers, and thinner. There was a cut across his forehead. His ribs jutted through the gown. Some were in two pieces. I checked his temperature, held his face with both hands like my mother used to hold mine. His blue eyes rolled around in the sockets. His skin felt icy, but that was common now in this city. All of them were cold, and getting clumsier in flight.

Downtown, more than one rather large, disoriented "bird," according to the *Times-Picayune*, has crashed into the side of a high-rise office building at dusk. They never write about the odd, purple blood spots or the claw marks that stretch for three stories down the side of the building, the six-foot long feathers slowly arcing their way to the sidewalk. Birds don't make that kind of noise. Birds don't scream like that. But these guys aren't supposed to exist anymore, and human denial is more powerful than any reality, even when that reality is flying headlong into your conference room window, screaming in anguish with a human face and a 20-foot wingspan.

This one was coming around, blinking and shaking his head. His wings obscured half of my car, draping over it to make a sort of impromptu featherbed.

"What happened?"

I winced.

Their voices are internal, like an echo in your head on multi-sonic levels, rippling up and down the decibel ladder at once, the equivalent of a thundering, sonorous shimmer. When they speak like this, it's all I can hear, and their voice resonates for moments afterward. The sound gets inside my head and won't leave.

"I think you jumped in front of my car."

He looked up and fixed his gaze on me then, eyes now a chilled cerulean ... and I was a bug under a microscope, my mind reduced to white noise. I could neither blink nor turn away, time stopped, and I felt a falling sensation. He diverted his eyes and mumbled, "Sorry."

Even in a broken-down state, they're more powerful than people can understand. This is what I know: The abilities we usually associate with select humans – ESP, remote viewing, cloaking, levitation, that sort of thing – are as natural as flight to them, and they have a sharpness and focus of mind that can literally stun, even kill, lesser beings. This one was hurt, so he was a psychic loose cannon. Best not to make eye contact, but I couldn't help myself. He looked like somebody I knew.

He rose to his full height and placed his hand atop my head. I felt a mild current pass through me, a mixture of sympathy and rock-bottom despair. His hand covered my entire head and I was conscious of him trying not to scratch me. He seemed better now, seemed to have forgotten about the broken ribs. The blood disappeared as I watched, and he softened his gaze, peered down at me, a small wrinkle between his arched, silver brows.

"You're not scared of me."

"No. Are you OK?"

He looked down, seemed surprised to find himself still in a body.

"I think so."

"Can you fly?"

He lifted his wings, tried to stretch them out to full span. Then he moved them back and forth a little, hunching up his shoulders, eyes closed in concentration.

"It hurts."

"Let me see."

He turned around. His left wing was ripped half off his back, and there were things that must have been ligaments hanging in clumps like a mass of tangled cable wires. Blood seeped down his back.

"You'd better sit down for a while."

He perched on the hood of my wrecked Honda like a grotesque obscene hood ornament, meditatively fanning his right wing back and forth. I sat on his left side, on the ground, keeping an eye on that left wing. I got comfortable and lit a cigarette, blew smoke toward the pool of light from the street lamp overhead. He was staring up at the sky. There was a new moon that evening, which meant I couldn't see anything, but he seemed to be searching for something, expecting something.

It was after three a.m. The few drivers that sped down Elysian Fields did not slow down, did not even glance as they passed this winged creature crouched on the hood of my car, spilling blood all over the paint. Denial is powerful.

The silence stretched for seconds, then minutes. After about five minutes, I leaned back and inspected his wing. It was better but still damaged. The bleeding had slowed down. It had already disappeared from my hood and the pavement. Just then, an NOPD cruiser rounded the corner and slowed down. A flashlight shone on him, then me. The cop sped up and drove off.

A strange noise shook me out of my thoughts. I looked up. He had lowered his head and closed his eyes. He was rocking slightly, hunched over. Once again, I didn't know what to do. He seemed so beyond my help. I cleared my throat and asked the inevitable:

"What's wrong?"

"What's wrong." It was not a question. "I am tired."

"Do you miss someone? Is that what you are doing, looking for someone, one of ... yours?"

"Some of us are trying to die. It's difficult."

"Why are you doing this? Why start dying now?"

"You people, you see what is in front of you, what is nearest to you. Most of you live in a very small world. We – we see everything. Now, the past, the future."

"What do you see? What is it? What's going to happen here?"

He sighed. Instead of answering me, he introduced himself. He told me his name was Aeron and that he had a twin named Aesop. He and Aesop had been keeping watch over the lower Garden District neighborhood and part of downtown for two hundred and twelve years. Aesop had stayed in the attic of a church uptown throughout the hurricane and in the days afterward. He had flown out over the flooded, desperate city at night and seen things he refused to speak of. After that, he was never the same. He started flying into oncoming trains, pulling up at the very last second. He drank two fifths of Jameson one night and soared so high that he half-landed, half-fell back to Earth covered in ice with his eyes frozen open, not breathing. Last month, he strapped a concrete traffic barrier to each leg with light stevedoring rope and then fell from the Crescent City Connection bridge into the Mississippi river, slicing his throat with a saw as he plummeted. Aeron was not here when it happened, but when Aesop died, Aeron said, it felt as if someone had shot him in the chest with a cannon.

The Mississippi has claimed countless lives, it seems, human and otherwise. After the storm, I spoke to a jittery man who said

246

he had seen helicopters with nets full of bodies hovering over the river, then dumping. More than one person has told me this story. However, this is a city where truth and myth intermingle and merge into one. After the storm, the national and local news downplayed, then outright denied rumors of gang rapes, murders, rape/murder combinations, grisly executions conducted behind abandoned stores in a deserted city. The nation wanted to believe that it wasn't happening, so it wasn't. The truth is what you decide upon, despite what your eyes tell you.

I looked at him. He was picking at something on his gown that looked like a mosquito. A raptor looped high overhead, then flew off toward downtown.

"So, what, you're diving under Hondas in Gentilly now? I thought you guys were supposed to be helping us. You scared the crap out of me tonight."

As I said it, I could hear how whiny I sounded. I wanted to tell him that I was sorry about his brother, that I knew what it meant to lose someone close. My childhood best friend committed suicide when we were 20, thirty painkillers and a bottle of whiskey. We were tight when we were young, two misfits in a rich, private elementary school, two kids who liked to draw cartoons and stole cigarettes from our dads. I saw him at a party two months before he did it. He confessed to me over a keg of beer that I was his first sexual fantasy. Then he wrapped himself in white Christmas lights and danced through the crowd. I never saw him alive again. Every time I see his older brother who looks exactly like him, my guts lurch. I still look for him downtown. I have to remind myself he isn't here any more. But this business with Aeron and his twin, this was a little different.

"I don't wish to scare you. I'm sorry I wrecked your car. You have to try to understand. We need your help, too, sometimes."

"But you knew that my car wasn't going to kill you. Why did you do it?"

"I don't know. I guess I was lonely. I knew you would talk to me."

We sat together in silence for a while. I smoked and sat with him, not sure what else to do, what to say. I was lonely, too, but I was also half-convinced I'd lost my mind, sitting here on the street talking to a suicidal angel in the middle of the night. He glanced at me from time to time, but mostly kept his eyes focused on the night sky. It was pitch black, no stars save for Polaris, that faithful, shimmering pinpoint.

"Aeron, what the hell are you looking for up there?"

"Reinforcements."

TRACKS
Katie Walenter

The roads were more sunken than usual. Or maybe my tuning fork of a nervous system was simply more sensitive to the regular old bumps. I rode, trying not to think about him and the fact that he was no longer here. I kept riding, lost in sadness, and before I knew it, I was deeper into the lower Ninth Ward than I had ever dared to go. I found myself on the movie set of a post-apocalyptic city. I rode faster, not wanting to see the zombies surely lurking behind rotten windows and door frames. I imagined the eyes of such zombies would be twice as sunken as these streets. To break the silence, I directed "Cut!" but the sound of my own timid voice did little to reassure me.

One house stopped me in my tracks. I skidded in the sandy sediment that the grimy waters of the canals had left behind. This house was on the corner, but I hadn't yet reached the cross street. The structured had collapsed upon itself and much of its guts spilled out onto the surrounding yard and grassy sidewalk. Now, I have always considered myself a sort of archaeologist, so I quickly forgot where I was and began digging. I found many interesting objects, including a coffee mug with a yellow tabby's face on it lying next to a full tube of Aim toothpaste. There was a much loved doll by its appearances, dirt smudged on its cheek and tattered dress, dragged around no doubt by some girl who called it her baby. And a few feet from there a deck of cards fanned out in triumph. A flush, maybe, or a straight, but laying face down. Instinctively I knew not to peek. I didn't want to disturb that game or tempt fate. A bird overhead squawked me back to real time. But before I left the place where time had stopped, it occurred to me that someone could have died in this house. I quickly jumped back on my bike. When I reached the cross street I turned right. My stomach hurt when I saw a black wreath hung on the door above the railroad-like sign drawn by the search-and-rescue team. Sure enough, underneath the FEMA-coded X read "3".

I had enough exploring for one day. My eyes were bleary from crying. Even on the ground it's hard to force one's self to remember that this is real. I can understand why so many people don't want to believe this really happened and is really happening. But as I high-tailed it out of there, behind every window of each twisted, stinking house peered a pair of eerie glowing eyes.

A half hour later, I was crossing the rough Press Street railroad tracks on Royal when I saw Tom sitting in between the iron rails fingering the wooden ties. I had often found him this way, tracing the grooves left by years of wear and delinquent pieces of hot coal. I too loved the smell of oil and coal mixed together, heated up by the blazing sun. If you worked in an office like I did, you couldn't help but be drawn to a task more physical and of the earth. The whole work of plodding transportation, close and heavy on the ground, appealed to me. I used to spend my days dreaming of being a hobo, knowing full well that the rocking of the train would put me to sleep, making the idea of becoming an engineer or conductor unthinkable. I'd take up the banjo and travel the world. Tom talked about joining me. One day, he said, we'd ride down here to Press Street and leave our bikes in the grass. We'd hop on when the train was backing up slowly and head on out of town to nowhere, without telling a soul. The sun was boiling my tan skin. When I looked back, Tom was gone. Too many mirages for one day, I decided to ride to Mimi's for a High Life with a lime.

I sat there watching a new bartender flirt with a man who was definitely from out of town, a contractor most likely. He was too eager and didn't know his place in our world. In her defense, she probably needed the tips and wasn't as picky as I was about whose company I'd keep. You can't be picky when you're new. You've got to start somewhere. After watching them in annoyance I was happy to see walk in a young guy who used to play the banjo on Frenchmen Street. He looked around, measured the same scene I saw and sat two seats away from me. He took off his crumpled brown hat. His hair was dark and curly. No sign of sweat. He nodded in hello. "Do you want to hear about a house?" I asked. He said okay. Before I got to the part about the wreath, after the deck of cards but before the baby doll, the bartender finally came over and took his order. Scotch and soda on the rocks. He seemed so relieved by the arrival of his drink that I didn't have the heart to tell him about the wreath. I made up some stuff about what else I found. He seemed to enjoy the archaeological dig we were together making mentally. When I found myself lacking for more lies, I really looked at him and could see he had lost people too and that he was tired. He drained his glass quickly, threw me a glance and said "You're the best thing that happened to me today," and got up to leave.

When the door didn't creak after him I wasn't surprised.

SAINT CLAUDE
Ed Skoog

Masden passed the time singing the alphabet song quietly as Mrs. Brocato talked about Patagonia. He turned her invisible, lining up her roundness with a classmate's lumpy head. He sang his song, substituting random letters for the exact order when he became stuck. He put his face very close to his desk. His desk smelled like lemons.

When Mrs. Brocato stopped lecturing and the other second-graders had settled into cutting and pasting, she called Masden to her desk. Her bracelets jingled as she motioned him to approach. Masden slid from his seat.

"I apologize for not bringing my scissors," he said.

"That's not why I've called you here," said Mrs. Brocato.

She held out a five dollar bill and whispered. "You're the only one I trust in here, Masden. Would you be a dear and run next door? I'm real hungry. This baby makes me hungry."

"What do you want?" he asked.

"You know, the usual."

"You're going to have to write it down," said Masden. "I forgot it."

She scribbled some words on the corner of a wide-lined pad, tore it off, and handed him her order. Her eyes were ravenous and Masden for a moment wondered if she would eat the note and start chewing on him next. Instead, she handed Masden the note and the five-dollar bill and shooed him away. "Make that old lady plastic-wrap it," she said. "And hurry back."

He left the classroom and paused outside the door, waiting for it to shut before letting the breath whoosh from his lungs. Sitting all day did not agree with him. Most of what Mrs. Brocato said seemed like gibberish, though he felt sorry that she had to work when she was liable to have a baby any moment. She had instructed him to keep her pregnancy a secret, but he never really spoke to anyone, nor they to him. He was small for his age, and ugly.

He folded the bill in his pocket and read the note. *One order Chs. Grts-w-Shrimp Gravy, 4 lnks HOT sausage, oh hell plus 2 strips Bacon, and one Egg Beater, over e-z thank you very much, keep the change.*

The hallway was empty. Masden jogged down three flights of stairs into the heat. He paused by the flagpole and looked back, expecting someone to come bounding after him. He didn't like this school. It wasn't where he went before the flood. No one liked this new school. No one liked the new kids. The new uniforms were the wrong colors. School was too far away from home—this wasn't his neighborhood. Sometimes he felt like he might just stop existing, turn into a cloud or a bush.

A young man in a torn army jacket walked past the schoolyard. An old man in a tight brown suit and red tie walked the other way. Standing there alone, Masden thought the school looked sad and empty. The playground was wrong without anyone playing on it. Masden hurried to cross the street.

He walked up to St. Claude Avenue. Everything was on St. Claude. The Rally's had reopened, which made him hopeful; the Rally's by his house up on Claiborne was still closed. Work trucks hurtled toward Chalmette. Masden walked along the storefronts and felt the traffic passing inches away.

Tina's Grill had two sides, one a grill, one a bar. Masden tried to enter through the bar side but couldn't open the door. He heard voices inside and pushed harder but the door didn't give. Through a scratch in the windowpane he saw the bright rays of a wall-mounted television. Cupping his hands around his eyes he saw more clearly, and leaped back when he saw himself on the screen. He looked up and saw a video camera perched above the door, following him. He stepped left, it pointed left.

A man opened the door, holding a plastic cup. The door shut behind him. The man adjusted his tie and peered down at Masden.

"Top of the morning," the man said.

"All right," said Masden.

"All right," the man said. "Shouldn't you be in, like, school?"

"I'm getting breakfast for Mrs. Brocato."

"Good boy."

A car appeared at the curb. The car was driven by a young woman, and the man stepped inside without a word to her. He gave Masden a slight wave and a curl of his mustachioed lip. Masden watched them go.

He tried the second door. To his surprise, it opened easily and closed behind him with a plywood thwack. The grill was connected to the bar by a pair of swinging doors toward the back, where in the kitchen a radio played a song with fiddles and a woman singing. Several young men sat at the long red tongue of a counter, sipping coffee from white mugs, turning pages of the *Times-Picayune*'s classifieds. They did not look up.

Tina cleared her throat and squinted at Masden, her red hair piled high atop her head like laundry.

"Can I get for ya?" she asked.

Masden handed her Mrs. Brocato's order and the five-dollar bill. Tina examined them. "Sit right here, honey," she said. "I'll get you some milk. I just have to make a little phone call first."

"Okay."

While he waited for Tina to bring him the milk, Masden eyed the unread sections of a newspaper a man was reading a few stools down. He knew the comics were in one of them, but he was afraid to grab the whole edition. He slid one seat closer to the paper.

"It's all yours, son," said the man reading the want ads. "This is the only part I need, not that it does much for me."

"Thank you, mister," said Masden.

"My advice to you, son, is learn a trade."

"I like the funnies."

"Stay in school. Find a path and follow it to glory."

"Yes, sir."

"And most importantly, son, stay clear of the horses."

"Thank you sir."

"Now that's enough," said Tina. "Here's your milk, honey."

Masden took a sip of milk and launched himself into the comics, examining the drawings inside each box. If the drawing was funny, like the fat man eating a turkey leg, he read the dialogue.

The plywood door thwacked again and the school principal, Dr. Jimmy Lunday, plopped down on the stool next to Masden.

"Hello, Masden," said Dr. Jimmy Lunday. "Are you ready to go back now?"

Masden nodded. He slurped the rest of the milk and they walked together toward the door.

"What about Mrs. Brocato's breakfast?" asked Masden.

"She'll get hers," said Dr. Lunday.

"See you later, Jimmy," yelled Tina as they left.

The two of them walked down St. Claude. Dr. Lunday held Masden's hand as they crossed St. Claude.

"What about Mrs. Brocato's baby?"

The principal loomed down. "Baby?"

Masden followed the principal's gaze in the direction of the open third-floor windows of Mrs. Brocato's classroom. "Masden, Mrs. Brocato is in her golden years. There's no baby in her future, I assure you. Now let's get inside. Would you do a favor for me, little man? Would you go see the counselor, Ms. Chang? At the end of the hall?"

Masden nodded and followed the principal until he went into his office. Masden looked down the hallway a moment, then turned around and ran out the door.

He ran for quite a while, fleeing at first but then running for the sake of running, enjoying the way fences and cars flew past him. He felt that nothing would harm him. But eventually the running began to hurt, and sharp pains emerged in his side. He slowed to a walk, then sat on a stoop.

He looked around. Wires spread like a canopy from houses to poles. Every parked car had a series of dents at the same level, and some tail lights were smashed or missing. One car, large and old as an uncle, had black tarp instead of glass for a driver's side window. The plastic flapped in the breeze. It was a lonely sound.

Everything was suddenly lonely. The heat was lonely, the sky was lonely, his loneliness was lonely. He took off his shoes and socks and each one of his toes looked individually lonely, but he felt

better with a slight breeze flowing over his feet. He had recently grown
a few hairs on the knuckles of his toes, and the way these bristled now
made him squirm, as if being tickled.

A naked woman walked out of her house across the street. She
was tall and her long hair, recently dried, frizzed around her shoulders.
She stood there squinting for a moment before checking her mailbox.
The sun made quarter-moon shadows under her breasts, and her pubic
hair was shaved into a neat triangle, like the face of a fox. She found
several pieces of mail and shuffled through, choosing one and sticking
the remainder in her armpit. With her long thumbnail, she sliced open
the letter. Masden could see handwriting on the yellow paper. The
woman began reading the letter and nodding her head. She turned and
walked back inside, still reading.

Masden wandered through the tall weeds of a vacant lot
between two shotgun houses. The weeds had burrs, and they burrowed
into Masden's pant cuffs and socks. When he reached the sidewalk on
the other side, he bent down to tweeze out the burrs between his thumb
and forefinger. Absorbed in the work, Masden was surprised to see a
white pick-up truck had sidled up to the curb. The doors opened and
two heavy and unshaven white men in blue tank tops stepped out. A
third man, with mirrored sunglasses, stayed behind the wheel.

"Hey little man," said one.

Masden lowered his eyes and picked a burr from his shoelace.
He heard his own heart speed up and tried to breathe slowly so they
couldn't tell.

"Little man, you got a thorn in your paw?"

Masden stood up. The tallest and heaviest of them peered down
the one-way street, looking for something. The one in white shorts
hopped in the back of the truck and lifted a Styrofoam cooler.

"You sure this is the address?" the tall one said. "I don't see a number."

"The exact address isn't important. We're not going inside," said White Shorts. "Keep your eye open. Johnny drives a purple van."

"We going to get these coolers back? I don't have coolers to give away, you know. Them coolers are expensive. Johnny has to figure in the coolers if he wants them."

"Come on, if Johnny wants the coolers, he gets the coolers."

White Shorts flipped open a cooler lid, reached in, and pulled out a dripping handful of shrimp and ice. He selected one shrimp and let the rest fall back to the cooler. He flicked it with his finger. "Hell, they're still good," he said to the third man, who had remained behind the wheel.

"All right," replied the third man in a froggy baritone.

Masden had moved close to a tree growing from the sidewalk, ready to race if one of the men suddenly lunged for him.

"Hey little man, maybe you can help us out with a little problem, uh? I'm supposed to meet my uncle here. We got all this shrimp to give to him. He drives a purple truck. Have you seen any purple trucks in the last few minutes?"

"It's a van," White Shorts called down.

"Little man, do you know the van of which we speak?" the tall man asked.

Masden shook his head.

"Shit," said the third man.

"Now now," said the tall man. He whistled and gestured to White Shorts. "Bag me up a pound of that shrimp for our friend here."

Masden stepped away from the tree towards the truck. "For me?"

"Sure. You're our pal, right? We're buds."

"Maybe he don't want the shrimp, Boo. Maybe he's allergic."

"Allergic to shellfish? Aw, that's too bad. Well take some home to your mama, then. We must always keep our mothers happy. Right, little man? What you think, one pound, two pound?"

"Shit," the third man repeated.

White Shorts handed down a plastic bag. Water dripped out where the shrimp's sharp heads poked through. "Here's three pounds. I bet he's got a great big family."

"Sure, give him three. We got plenty of shrimp to spare."

The tall man and White Shorts laughed, then the third man suddenly started laughing too. "We got plenty of shrimp, that's true!"

Masden looked in the heavy bag. The shrimps were long, thick and dead, their pinpoint black eyes without any luster. He'd never seen shrimp with the head and feet attached. They looked strange, these little cadavers. The smell reminded him of those days on the roof, the poo water that floated away their car. The water they walked through, on the third day, to the Shell station, and the fourth day to his old elementary school, and its roof where the helicopters took them to the airport, where the airplane took them to Utah.

He closed the shrimp bag and thanked the three men. They had already forgotten him.

Masden continued down Chartres Street with his bag of shrimp. He walked along the flood wall that held back the

Mississippi River. A large ship sounded its horn. He saw its smokestacks pass over the wall, round and painted pink like giant birthday cakes.

He settled under a tree on the slope between the walls and the road. He rustled through the sack and picked out a particularly thick shrimp. Its eyes were tiny, like seeds. He pinched the head and twisted and pulled until it came away from the body. He threw the head into the high weeds, sure some animal there, snake or rat, would appreciate the gift. He ran his thumbnail along the underside of the tail, creasing the soft transparent belly-shell, then pulled at the ridge as if opening a bible. Masden squeezed the flesh from the tail and ate it in two bites.

He started walking again. Sweat expanded like shadows from his armpits and from the small of his back. He darted from shade tree to store awning. He wished he was home, stripped to his drawers in front of an electric fan, a porcelain bowl of ice cubes on his lap.

He looked around for a familiar landmark and found none. He was certain he'd never seen the church he passed, a whitewashed church with cracks in the steps. He crossed a series of railroad tracks and couldn't imagine where they came from or where they led.

Thunderheads growled in the sky, with lightning making distant faces in the gray recesses of the clouds. The idea of rain, along with the saltiness of the shrimp made him want a glass of water.

A corner grocery appeared, its walls painted yellow, its roof leaning severely over the sidewalk. He asked for water and the old woman behind the counter gave him a small plastic bottle of Coke.

Her husband started to protest but the woman smiled and asked if he was lost.

"I guess I am, ma'am," said Masden. He drank his Coke in several gulps and felt woozy.

"It's the carbonation," said the old woman. "Let yourself burp."

"Ma'am?"

"Just do it."

Masden leaned back and let his body open into a ripping belch that stung his throat.

"That's better, isn't it? I had ten children, I know how to fix them."

The husband rolled his eyes and wandered into the back room.

"Now where are you from?"

Masden told her.

"Oh my you're a long way from home." The old woman told Masden where to find the bus and gave him another Coke. He took a sip and made himself burp again.

"Music to my ears," said the woman.

Masden didn't have money for the bus, but he followed the old woman's directions. He didn't seem to be making any headway. He was more tired than he could remember feeling before. His feet hurt and his neck was sunburned. He was on St. Claude Avenue again, according to the sign, but it was a stretch unfamiliar to him. There were more houses and fewer pawn shops. He saw a health clinic and a sit-down restaurant. He tried to figure out where the buses were going, but he didn't want to walk a hundred miles in the wrong direction, following the wrong bus. His side hurt like being stabbed, and the blisters on his heel felt like burns. He leaned against a crepe myrtle tree and slid to the ground. He closed his eyes.

264

"Hey little man," said a rough voice.

Masden woke up. The sun was lower in the sky but it was still hot. Masden looked around and saw the white truck of the men who'd given him the shrimp.

"You need a ride, little man?"

Masden tried to say no but couldn't speak, his throat was so dry. He nodded and White Shorts gestured for him to climb in the back. He gave Masden an enthusiastic thumbs-up and the truck lurched forward. Ice rattled in chests, and the chests themselves moved around. Masden worried that they might crush him, but he just lay there, flush against their cool sides.

Amanda Anderson lives and writes in a rural hideaway in Mid-City, New Orleans. Now that AOL has pulled the plug on her blogging website, www.bloggingneworleans.com, she plans to croak out the occasional entry for NOLAFugees.com and finally write her motherfucking novel instead of just talking about it.

Jason Berry's latest book, *Last of the Red Hot Poppas* (2006, Chin Music Press) is a comic novel about Louisiana politics. For his investigative reporting on the Catholic clergy sex abuse crisis he has made many national media appearances. *Lead Us Not Into Temptation* (1992) is still used in many newsrooms. *Vows of Silence: The Abuse of Power in the Papacy of John Paul II* (2004) written with Gerald Renner, has Italian, Spanish and Australian editions. Berry is directing a film documentary based on the book. He received a Guggenheim Fellowship for jazz funerals research and an Alicia Patterson Journalism Fellowship for reporting on demagogues. His play *Earl Long in Purgatory*, won a Big Easy award for Best Original Work in Theatre.

Berman Black's work has appeared under various pseudonymns in publications such as the *Mississippi Review* and *Opium*. He currently works as a construction manager for a non-profit in New Orleans and is the Associate Director of Press Street, a literary and visual arts 501(c)3 out of the Bywater.

Andrea Boll is rebuilding in New Orleans.

Justin Burnell is 25 years old and lives in New Orleans.

Tara Jill Ciccarone holds it down in the Faubourg Marigny where she's working on a collection of short stories about a neighborhood spiraling out of control into a whirlwind of drugs and alcohol after Hurricane Katrina. She's learned her lesson and is currently single.

Lucas Díaz-Medina, born in Santo Domingo, Dominican Republic, immigrated as a child with his parents to Louisiana in 1977. He completed his BA in creative writing from Loyola University New Orleans and his MFA in creative writing from the University of New Orleans. Mr. Díaz-Medina works in the New Orleans area and is the author of *Passing Unseen: Stories from New Domangue*, a collection of short stories set in a fictional town south of New Orleans. He received positive reviews from *The New York Times* and *The Chicago Tribune* for his fictional narrative of Strange Fruit, Irvin Mayfield's 2005 epic jazz release, as well as from *All About Jazz* for Mr. Díaz-Medina's album notes on the 2005 Los Hombres Calientes release, *Volume 5: Carnival*. He is currently working on a novel.

Joel Farrelly's main contribution as a writer has been in the form of sequential art scripts ("or comic books if you want to be all judgmental about it"). He attended the New Orleans Center for Creative Arts where he studied film theory and creative writing and is currently pursuing his Master's in English at U.N.O. He was born in New Orleans, Louisiana in 1984 and has yet to shed his unrequited love for this city, although Joel has "been forced" to take up residence in Metairie since Katrina.

Ken Foster is the author of *The Dogs Who Found Me*, a memoir; *The Kind I'm Likely to Get*, a collection of stories; and *Dogs I Have Met*, essays. His work has appeared in *Fence, McSweeney's, The Believer, Salon, The Village Voice, The New Orleans Times-Picayune, The San Francisco Chronicle* and elsewhere. He and his dogs live in the beautiful lower Ninth.

Patty Friedmann is the author of six darkly comic literary novels set in New Orleans: *The Exact Image of Mother, Eleanor Rushing, Odds, Secondhand Smoke, Side Effects*, and *A Little Bit Ruined* as well as the humor book *Too Smart to Be Rich*. Her titles have been chosen as Discover Great New Writers, Original Voices, and Book Sense 76 selections. Her stage pieces have been part of Native Tongues. With slight interruptions for education and natural disasters, she always has lived in New Orleans.

Kelly Gartman is a writer and artist who has lived in New Orleans for a total of seven years. She received an MFA in Poetry from the University of New Orleans in 2004. She currently works for the Department of Defense as a technical writer.

Anne Gisleson teaches at the New Orleans Center for Creative Arts, Louisiana's arts conservatory for high school students, which is a four-minute walk from her Bywater home where she lives with her two wonderful sons and her incredibly talented husband, artist Brad Benischek and where Press Street, a literary and visual arts collective which publishes books and hosts art events meets weekly in her kitchen. She's published poetry, fiction and non-fiction in various places.

Dana Harrison-Tidwell's poetry, fiction, essays and articles have appeared in numerous literary and news journals, magazines and e-zines (including NOLAfugees.com), as well as in the poetry collection, *Velvet Avalanche*. She is the editor of a women's lifestyle magazine, and is a regular contributor to several other Southwestern food, design and lifestyle magazines. Dana is the publisher and editor of, as well as primary writer for, the *diva in a carry on* travel blog, and is currently focusing her attention on travel writing. She holds an MFA in Creative Writing from the University of New Orleans, and in spite of her physical location, considers the French Quarter her home.

Sarah K. Inman has worked as a park ranger, boxer, aerialist and department chair. Livingston Press published her first novel, *Finishing Skills* in 2005. Her writing has appeared in such publications as *Louisiana in Words*, *Do You Know What It Means to Miss New Orleans*, and *Tied in Knots: Funny Stories from the Wedding Day*. She contributes regularly to NOLAFugees.com. "The Least Resistance" is an excerpt from a novella set during the aftermath of the storm.

Leonard Earl Johnson is winner of the Press Club of New Orleans Award for Excellence, and the Key to The City and Certificate of Appreciation from City Council. He is a columnist at *Les Amis de Marigny, New Orleans*, and *African-American Village*. Also a contributor to *ConsumerAffairs.com, Gambit Weekly, New Orleans Magazine, SCAT, Baton Rouge Advocate, The Times-Picayune*, and the books *French Quarter Fiction* and *Louisiana In Words*. He attended Southern Illinois University, Carbondale, and Harry Lundberg School of Seamanship, Piney Point, Maryland. His web site is www.LEJ.org

Karissa Kary's work has appeared in *Louisiana In Words*. She has worked as Associate Director for the Tennessee Williams/New Orleans Literary Festival. She currently lives in Brazil.

Jennifer A. Kuchta teaches creative writing, literature, and composition at the University of New Orleans. Her non-fiction has appeared most recently in *Year Zero: A Year of Reporting From Post-Katrina New Orleans* and on NOLAFugees.com. Her fiction has been published in *Ellipsis*, *Rive Gauche* and *The Southern Anthology*. Kuchta is hard at work on her novel, Allegiance, and still makes her home in Uptown, New Orleans with four dogs, a deaf cat, and a raggedy Cadillac.

Kris Lackey teaches at the University of New Orleans. He is the author of *Roadframes: The American Highway Narrative* and a number of short stories, in *Missouri Review*, *Wisconsin Review*, and other literary magazines.

Bill Lavender is a poet living in New Orleans or, since Katrina, thereabouts. His books include *look the universe is dreaming* (Potes and Poets, 2002), *While Sleeping* (Chax, 2004), and *I of the Storm* (Trembling Pillow, 2006).

Andy Levin is a former contributing photographer for *Life*. His photojournalism has appeared in most major publications in the US and around the world. His personal b/w reportage on Coney Island has been published in numerous prestigious camera magazines including *Graphis* and *Reportage*. In 2004, after living in New York City for more than 20 years, he moved to New Orleans. Levin documented the culture of the city a year before Hurricane Katrina, then documented the storm and its aftermath, photographing as he helped evacuate neighbors from their Mid-City homes. His work is available at the website www.andylevin.com.

Bill Loehfelm was born in Park Slope, Brooklyn in 1969. In 1997, he moved to New Orleans' Garden District where he lives with his lovely wife, award-winning fiction writer AC Lambeth. Loehfelm's post-K non-fiction has appeared in *Year Zero: A Year of Reporting from Post-Katrina New Orleans*, and in Bergen County,

New Jersey's *Courier-News*. His short fiction has appeared in several journals. Loehfelm enjoys writing about islands, real and imagined. They are the subjects of his two novels.

Ed Skoog taught at New Orleans Center for Creative Arts/Riverfront from 2000-2005. His first book of poems, *Mister Skylight*, will be published by Copper Canyon Press in 2009.

Katie Walenter is a New Orleans writer living in San Francisco with Sam the NOLA cat. She currently spends her time reading sidewalk graffiti and talking to old men in dive bars.

ABOUT NOLAFUGEES.COM

NOLAFugees.com was conceived as a response to the national media coverage of the flooding of the Crescent City. After witnessing the gross inaccuracies that served to document the greatest natural disaster in American history, we decided we'd try our hands at chronicling life in the wake of the storm.

We began publication in November of 2005 as a bi-weekly online magazine documenting life in New Orleans in the immediate aftermath of Hurricane Katrina, ranging from the surreal to the peculiar to the gravely serious.

Since then we have expanded our pool of talented writers and the range of topics we cover around the city and to points beyond. Our content includes political and social commentary, coverage of local music and culture, iconoclastic first-person essays, and our trademark sharp and controversial satire that "blurs the lines" between fact and fiction in New Orleans.

Our mission is to provide another record of life in New Orleans, one that exists beyond the mainstream news, the alternative weeklies, the guidebooks and tourist commercials. We are advocates for the city as it is, not the city as it is branded. Our New Orleans is wild, dangerous, and random. It is a city of great possibilities and of great failures. It is a city unlike any other.

WWW.**NOLAF**UGEES.COM

Made in the USA
Lexington, KY
19 April 2015